MASON

Bachelors Incorporated, Book 1

ALLISON LAFLEUR

Edited by
KATE DOWNS

Summer Storm PUBLISHING

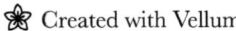

Chapter One

KINSEY

HEIRESS DRUNK AND OUT OF CONTROL
SPOTTED AT FRAT PARTY ORGY
WHAT WILL SHE DO NEXT?

*M*y unflattering image caught me by surprise as I unfolded the morning paper. My bleary eyes blinked, stunned, as I read the front page article that would have been more at home in a tabloid. My bloodshot eyes from studying for three days made me look drunk and high. Carlyn flanked one side of me and Matty the other, so they appeared to be supporting me instead of the other way around. In reality, I dragged them out mere moments before the police arrived.

My stomach churned and bile rose in my throat. I stood there, door open and worried what my father would say at lunch. A total klutz my entire life, the tabloids always seemed to catch me at my worst. This was no exception— there I was in black and white, in one of my oldest and softest t-shirts, a pair of cut off jean shorts, cheap rubber flip flops with my

1

hair a rats nest on top of my head. I looked nothing like my normal put together self.

sigh

DING!

I glanced down to see a text from my father.

We need to talk. —Dad

Shit! He must have seen the photo. I closed my eyes, slightly dizzy from lack of sleep and realized the nap I had been looking forward to was not going to happen. My finals were over, but my day it seemed was not.

DING!

Expecting it to be my dad again, I closed the front door of my apartment and cautiously peered at my phone only to see a message from my credit card company.

555-222

AMEX: Please call the number on the back of your card ASAP to discuss spending over the set limit.

I rubbed my eyes, sure I was hallucinating. I hadn't been anywhere except the library and my dorm for the last week. It was not possible to be over my limit.

Fine.

I leaned back against the closed door and walked over to my computer, dropping the offending paper on the coffee table on my way.

Sliding into my chair, I leaned forward on my elbows, supporting my head as I logged in to my Amex account.

When the cursor finally stopped spinning and the login page appeared, I gasped. Dozens of charges scrolled across the page. Bergdorf's, Louis Vuitton, Armani... Armani? Wait a minute. I reached for my phone to call Jason when speak of the devil, he waltzed in the door, laden with shopping bags.

"Hey babe!" He kissed my cheek, dropped the bags on the

floor and fell back into my leather couch. "I had the best day, I took the boys shopping."

"What? How?" Jason worked haphazardly and never had money. A little slow on the uptake, I hadn't made the connection yet.

"Here!" He leaned forward and rummaged in the coach bag. He emerged triumphantly holding a small coach bag aloft. "I got you something."

Dumbly, I opened it to reveal a small coach wristlet, inside of which my Amex shone from one of the pockets.

"Dammit Jason! You took them shopping with my card??!!!"

He leaned back. "I knew you wouldn't mind. It's not like you'll miss the money."

"Jason!" I gritted my teeth and let out a groan. "I've told you my dad keeps me on a budget. You took me over my limit!"

"Pshhhhh, you're daddy's little girl. You'll smile and he'll forgive you."

"Not this morning he won't, look!" I held up the newspaper.

"Oh look! The Packers drafted that rookie!" He snatched the paper and flipped to the sports section, completely ignoring me.

I bit my tongue for a moment, before snatching the paper from him. "He's already pissed, and I didn't even go to that damn party. Jason, you've got to stop taking my card, he can't see bills like this!"

"Relax babe. Look, I'll come back when you're not so pissy." He stood, grabbing his bags and ambling out, leaving me to clean up his mess.

Why did I always date immature assholes?

The night before...

R *ING RING*
"Hello?" I swiped a strand of blond hair out of my face, my eyes so tired, they threatened to flutter closed any second. After three days of cramming I was almost ready for my biochem midterm.

"Kinsey!"

"I can hardly hear you, it's so noisy."

"Kinsey, you've gotta come get us." Carlyn's words were so slurred I could barely understand her, but I knew what she needed. "It's, it's… The guys got into some bad stuff, they're fighting, some girls are crying, we gotta get out of here." This wasn't the first time I'd had to bail her and Matty out of some uncomfortable situation in the middle of the night. We had been friends since preschool, and I knew they would do the same for me.

For Carlyn and Matty, college was about the parties and the boys. I think Carlyn's major was something like Entertainment and Recreation in the 21st century. A degree that was designed to net her a husband, not a job.

"Where are you?" I blew air out my nose, a strand of hair flopping in front of my eye. I sat up to stretch the kinks out of my back and shoved the stack of open textbooks, to the foot of my bed. The three hours of sleep I had hoped to catch before my test were now out of the question.

"Alpha Psi house. Someone just said the neighbors called the cops. Everyone is panicking, please hurry!" She hiccuped.

Chapter Two

MASON

*S*niff

 "Gah!" Lily was cute, but boy, did her vomit smell.

I unbuttoned my soiled shirt, pulled open the bottom desk drawer, and pulled out a clean button down still folded in the plastic dry cleaning bag. Quickly changing, I logged into my computer and started sifting through my email. At 8 pm, while the rest of New York was heading out clubbing or off to see a Broadway show, I was settling in for a long night of work.

I had an unusual number of messages from my onsite manager in China. Clicking on the first email, I started to read.

Mason, big problems. Call me.

I checked the time. It was 8am in China. He'd still be reachable.

Mason, huge issues. Production is going to be

delayed. CALL ME!

Each message grew more insistent. I scrolled down, scanned the list, and reached for the phone. Carl had a messaged me every five minutes.

What the hell is going on in China?

"Mason! Thank God you called!" Carl's panicked voice came across the line. "It's a disaster here. We're already a week behind schedule."

I could barely understand him. "Slow down, Carl. What's going on?"

"Half the workers have called out sick, the other half has shown up dead on their feet, and the assembly line is a mess. There's a group picketing out front, calling for an overhaul of the Chinese workers' rights system. The police are everywhere. Everyone is working scared. There's no way to meet our deadlines!"

"Carl—Carl, calm down. What are the workers sick with?"

"I don't know. Bird flu, maybe? They're running fevers and vomiting. The factory stinks!"

"Ok, ok. We can deal with this. They can't work sick. Pay them all for the next three days. Send them home. Get a cleaning crew in there. We can't make these video cards in a dirty factory. Have the crew disinfect and sterilize everything."

"That will put us further behind!" Carl protested.

"It will be okay. When we get back up and running, we'll work around the clock and split everyone into three shifts for a few weeks to make up for lost time." My mind raced. This disaster was going to put a serious wrinkle in the marketing of my video card. A breakthrough for the industry, we were already touting it as the next generation in gaming graphics. It had to be ready in time.

∾

S unlight streamed through a gap in the blinds and woke me shortly after sunrise. Tangled up in my silk sheets, I rolled onto my back and scratched my stomach, my hand idly tracing the line of dark hair leading south from my belly button. I stretched and yawned, rolled out of bed and rubbed the stubble on my chin. *I really need to shave.* I had fallen asleep surrounded by contracts sometime after 3 am. I needed to get back at it.

I grabbed my pajama pants from the back of a chair where I'd tossed them the night before, and pulled them on before padding out of the master bedroom, and into the kitchen. One time, I'd made the mistake of wandering out there naked on a day the cleaning lady was scheduled. I had never heard anyone scream so loudly in my life.

Ding!

My phone. With a sigh, I changed direction to where I'd left it charging on the kitchen counter. *I guess it's time to start the day.*

Mom: Don't forget dinner at Mark's at five.
Ding!
Mom: Bring wine.
Ding!
Mom: Don't be late!
Me: Yes, Mom.

I rolled my eyes. Some days, I think she forgets I'm a grown man. She's a great mom and a strong, determined woman. She had to be, to raise two rambunctious boys after losing Dad so early, but she did it, and she saved his patents. I would never be able to make up for those early years.

The smell of coffee wafting through the condo, tore me away from my musings, as I gazed out at the dawn sky spreading across the waking city.

My condo reflected me; it was my sanctuary. Walking into the living room, a wall of glass stretched from one side to the other. There were no curtains or blinds between me and the new day. I'd designed the office building the same way. I don't like things separating me from the rest of the world. I get my best ideas looking out and over the bustling chaos of New York City.

I followed the enticing aroma of coffee back to the kitchen, imagining that first scalding sip of precious brew as my eyes fell across the photographs decorating the walls. The stark, clean black and white lines were reminiscent of Ansel Adams or Clyde Butcher. My photos were a glimpse into how I saw the world.

I started taking pictures with my dad's old Hasselblad camera when I was a teenager. At first it was a way to be closer to him, but then I started to like it. My high school and college photography teachers all told me I had a good eye and encouraged me to exhibit and sell my work, but I preferred to keep it private. I gave copies of my best photos to Mark and Mom, but most of it was there on the walls just for me. Photography brought me peace.

When I needed to work out a problem, I would pull on my old leather jacket, throw a ball cap on my head, grab my camera, and roam the streets of New York. If something caught my eye, I would explore the lines and textures through the camera lens. Usually by the end of the night, whatever problem my brain was working on would have worked itself out, and I would have a couple amazing shots to celebrate with back home in my safe space.

I didn't bring women here. If I decided to go home with a woman, we went to her place. That way there was no awkwardness getting her to leave in the morning. There were no expectations of waking up together, no confusion about long-term relationships.

I really liked my life. There was no need to change.

Chapter Three

KINSEY

Present

I hit the brakes, tires squealing, the rear of the car fishtailing as my mini rolled to a stop halfway to dad's office.

I leapt out, stopping just a few feet away from the bloody animal cowering in the gutter.

"Here, puppy." I crouched down on the side of the road, one hand out palm up, the other fishing in my bag for anything that might entice him closer. "Here, boy."

Slowly, the animal slunk up, a paw in the air, limping, tail between its legs.

"You haven't had a very good day have you?" I sang to him.

Shaking, the pup sniffed my hand. I used an old McDonald's cup, tearing the top half off and filling it with water from a Nalgene water bottle. He drank thirstily.

My eyes took in the dried blood around the shoulder, the crooked paw held up by its chest, and I cried. I glanced at my watch. I would be late, but I couldn't just leave it here. Some asshole must have hit it and fled.

"That's it, drink up." I cautiously ran my hand across the top of his head, careful not to touch any sore spots. "Ok, boy, we need to get you to a vet."

I stood, taking two steps to the car and pulling a blanket from the back, and wrapped it around the dog, who docilely let me pick him up and lay him on the front seat.

"You just lay there, we'll be there in no time."

I slid in to the driver's seat and pulled out my smartphone, googling vet offices.

I stepped out onto the sidewalk and shut the car door, handing the valet my keys. I knew I was late, but I still took a moment to gaze up at New York City as it reflected back at me in the mirrored glass of Hendrix BioTech's headquarters. I wanted to work for that company one day. I was studying biochemistry and engineering in the hopes Dad would change his mind about not involving me in the business.

Hitching my purse and backpack up higher on my shoulder, I took a deep breath and mustered all the courage I had. I knew he'd be waiting in his office, angry and barking orders at his latest executive assistant.

Time to face the music. Trying to wipe some of the blood off the front of my shirt, I strolled through the double glass doors with my head held high. I walked straight past the security desks, into the elevator, and up to dad's office. Ignoring everyone. I didn't have time for pleasantries, I knew he needed my help today and I was running two hours behind.

"You're late, Kinsey. Where have you been?" Frost dripped from his voice as I entered. Dad put down the report he'd been reading and turned his silver streaked head to address me like I was a rival business associate. Yep, he was pissed. He had seen the headline. I just mentally hoped he hadn't seen the credit card bill.

I sighed. "Hi, Dad." I walked toward him as he stood and stretched up on my tiptoes to air kiss both of his cheeks. "I am so sorry I'm late. There was a tiny problem on the way here. I... um... well, there was a dog... and well, I'm sorry I'm late." My face reddened in embarrassment.

He completely ignored the apology. "Kinsey, it's time for you to grow up and quit playing around. Look at today; you can't even show up on time. And you're filthy. And that head-line!" His voice dripped with disapproval as he held up the offending front page. I felt like I was ten again and had just spilled grape juice on the Persian carpet.

"What they hell were you playing at last night. How could you let them photograph you? Do you know stocks have slipped 100 points this morning? How the hell do you think I can pay your outrageous credit card bills if you do things to tank the company?"

Oh shit, he had seen the credit card charges. "It won't happen again," I whispered, looking down at my feet. "I'm sorry, I didn't think anyone saw me. I just went to pick them up."

"You're right. It won't happen again." He sighed, rubbing the tension lines in his forehead. "I don't care why you were there. No one does, they like headlines, and you make it easy."

"I'm sorry Dad, what can I do?"

"First of all, you can get a job and pay that ridiculous credit card bill. I'm done bailing you out." He sat back down. "And secondly, I needed your Mandarin skills this morning and you let me down. You know you're better on the phone than I am. Ambassador Zao and I stumbled through, but it took three times as long as it should have. And why? Because you weren't here on time!"

"I... I can call him back!"

"Too late, I have another meeting in ten minutes. Maybe next time you can be here when I tell you to." He picked up the report he'd set down when I'd walked in. "I've already arranged with my assistant to bring me a sandwich. At least *she* can keep a schedule."

~

MASON

The elevator doors opened, and so lost in thought I stepped in without looking and ran right into an emerging lithe, blond bundle of angry energy.

"Oof!" I heard her take a quick breath. I looked down to find a pair of big blue eyes staring up at me. My arms wrapped around her soft, curvy body to keep her from falling. With her nose buried in my chest, I enjoyed the soft, sweet smelling woman pressed up against me.

"Hi there." I watched as she freed herself from my arms. "Can I help you?" My eyes danced at her predicament.

"Oh! I am so sorry." She gasped and laughed with me.

Carefully, I set her on her feet, far enough away from me so I couldn't feel her lush body or smell her faint, intoxicating perfume. She was the kind of woman that could get a man in trouble.

"I'm Mason," I started to say, grinning. She was attractive, and even with her curves, looked athletic. *Maybe I should ask her out.* Despite her upset, she was cute in her yoga pants and loose top, even with, wait, *is that blood???*

"I'm Kinsey," she said, brushing her hair out of her eyes. She took a step back and tucked a lock of golden blond hair behind a perfectly-shaped ear.

At the sound of her name, I stilled. *Kinsey? This can't be*

Kinsey! "Noah's Kinsey?" Even as I asked the question, I knew it had to be her.

Two deep blue pools swimming with unshed tears peered up at me. I knew those eyes, although the body they were attached to had changed. It had grown lush, with round curves packed into a dynamite package. *This can't possibly be Kinsey!*

"Yes. Do I know you? Wait… Mason?" Her eyes widened, the tears threatening to spill over. Hitching her bag up on her shoulder, she sniffed and blinked rapidly. "Sorry. It's been a really bad day, but… you look like you're in a hurry. Do you have time to catch up?"

"No. I've got to finish these contracts. I've got somewhere to be, then I'll be at my desk all afternoon."

"Oh, ok, well it was great to see you Mason." She dashed a hand across her eyes. "I really screwed up."

"Good luck," I said, wishing I had some wise words to offer. "Give me a holler later this afternoon, and we can catch up."

"That would be really great, I'll call you… what's a good time?"

"I should be back by three. What's up?"

"I need some advice, you were always good at that. Life is just… out of control, and now, I need to pay my dad back." She broke off, as if she'd said too much.

"Call me. We can talk it through. And I'll check with my administrative assistant. Maybe there is something you can do around my office. We always need help."

"Thank you, Mason." She gave me a quick hug. "I can't believe it's been so long since I've seen you."

I nodded and I quietly berated myself for the smile I couldn't hide. Noah would not be pleased. I had forgotten how breathtaking she was. It had been a few years, and the gangly teen had turned into a swan. I took one last lascivious look at her body and told myself I couldn't go there. What a pity she was Noah's daughter.

~

"Mason!" A tiny redheaded bundle of energy slammed into my knees, wrapped its arms around my legs, and held on tight. "You came back!"

Kneeling down, I wrapped her in a big hug. "Hi, Molly. How are you, munchkin?"

"The teacher says I can pass out the snacks today!"

"How exciting! You behaving yourself?" I ruffled her hair and stood. The lunch line would be opening in just a few minutes.

"Maaas-on!" She rolled her eyes at me and put her hands on her hips. A twenty-five year old looked up at me through a five-year old's eyes. "I'm gonna go tell Mom you're here. It's lunchtime!" And just like that, she scampered off, leaving me standing in the hallway.

On Fridays, I always went and served lunch at the women's shelter, and today was no exception. I still remember the year we lived there after dad died, and the tiny room the three of us had shared. The rules, the curfews, the sadness that permeated the building stayed with me.

My 5000-square-foot apartment was bigger than the whole shelter and situated in the most expensive part of New York City. I slept on 1800-count sheets, instead of stiff, thread-bare ones. Yet, I'd never forgotten how hard our time in that shelter was. I volunteered every week to keep me grounded.

None of the residents paid any attention to who I was, and I never volunteered my identity. I was just Mason. Not Mason Alexander, People magazine's most eligible billionaire bachelor two years running. I was just a guy who came to help.

This was a personal project. After I'd made my first billion, I had anonymously donated enough money to completely remodel and expand the shelter. Now, it had space for twice as many families and provided a full-time school teacher. Life doesn't offer a whole lot of stability when you're homeless, and I'd lost almost a year of schooling as we moved around. This was my way of trying to give back to the place that had provided a homeless, fatherless kid a modicum of stability in his screwed-up young life.

Chapter Four

MASON

Ding!

The box for the inter-office messenger popped up on my screen, providing a brief distraction from the China problems. *Why is Mary messaging me at this hour?*

> **Mary**: Mason, sorry to interrupt your evening, but I saw you were online. I need to take some time off. My mother fell and broke her hip.

Shit! Mary was the glue that held me together. She was my executive assistant, and I couldn't do without her. Part mother, part secretary, part sounding board, she ran the office with an iron fist. When my creativity took over and I buried myself in the design and development department, she made sure I was on time and attending my meetings. She was the reason I didn't miss deadlines. She saw to it that everyone who worked for me was taken care of and happy. She sent birthday cards, get well cards, baby shower gifts, and signed my name to everything I didn't have time for. She quietly explained to my 'girlfriends' that I was married to the company, and ordered them lovely parting gifts from Tiffany's. *What am I going to do without her?*

Me: Don't worry about us here. We can handle it. Take as much time as you need and take care of your mom.
Mary: She will be in the hospital for a few weeks. I'm going to fly up this weekend and meet with her doctors. I'll be back Tuesday to get things in order and find a temp for you.
Me: I'll let HR know they will be hearing from you.
Mary: Don't worry, Mason. I'll train someone before I leave. We have time.

This is a disaster! How the hell will I survive without Mary? Her counsel was invaluable. She would know how to fix this China problem and have it smoothed over with investors and buyers in no time.

Good God, I don't want to train someone new!

I glanced down at my cell, willing it to ring. Maybe running into Kinsey today was divine intervention.

And just like that the screen lit up.

Would Kinsey take a temporary job? I was about to find out.

I walked up the stone path to Mark's house, admiring his cozy home and thinking about Kinsey. It was the complete opposite of the tiny cracker box overlooking a four story fire escape they had first lived in.

"Helloooo?" I called, peering through the partially open front door.

"Mason!" Mark came around the corner with a kitchen towel tossed over his shoulder and barbecue tongs in hand. "I didn't think you would make it!" He hollered, "Hey, Mom! Mason's here!"

"Mark, hush! You'll wake the kids!" Laurie's admonishment came too late, and a low wail echoed over the baby monitor on the kitchen counter.

Waaaaaaaaaah! Waaaaaaaaaaah!

She smacked Mark on the butt with a dish towel and stomped up the stairs in a huff. "You woke them. I should make you take diaper duty!"

"Love you too, hon!" Mark called up the stairs at her retreating back.

"I want my burger medium-rare!" she said.

"You got it, babe! One medium-rare burger coming right up!" He grabbed two beers from the fridge and handed one to me. Mark gestured a 'follow me' with his tongs as he strutted out through the kitchen and back to the grill. "Come on. You can help me finish dinner. She'll be hungry after feeding the twins."

I could hear Laurie talking to the kids over the baby monitor. For a brief moment, I wondered what my life would be like if I had a family to come home to. Would it be different with a wife to snuggle up to on the couch after a long day? Would I be happier having a loved one to discuss the day's happenings with, a warm body to curl around— and groan together with when the kids woke us in the middle of the night? Could love bring me something I didn't already have?

Then I remembered—I was married to my work. *How would I fit a wife and kids into my sterile condo and the ridiculous number of hours a week I spend working?*

Mark seemed happy, though.

"Hey Mason, come here." My mom stood at the sliding doors with an armful of wriggling twin on one hip. I followed the stone walkway leading from the grill to the house, "Yeah, Mom? What do you need?"

"Hold Lily for me." She thrust the little girl into my arms. "I need to warm up a bottle for her. Laurie is nursing Lucas."

"Wait, what?" I awkwardly took the baby from my mother and held her out in front of me. Her little legs dangled, and she chewed on one fist with her bright eyes fixed on me. I looked at my mom and then back at Lily. *What exactly do you do with a baby?*

"Really, Mason?" She glanced over her shoulder and rolled her eyes at me. "Here." She came back with a luke-warm bottle. "Like this." Mom tucked Lily into my arms like a football and thrust the bottle into my hand. "She's hungry."

I felt totally out of my element. I was used to holding cell phones and ink pens—that's when the magic happened for me. Holding an infant who trusted me to take care of all her needs? To feed and protect her? That wasn't something I was good at.

My mother stood behind me, leaning over my shoulder and making silly faces at the baby as I gave Lily her bottle. "Relax, Mason. She won't break." Mom put her hand on my shoulder. "You can do this."

The warm weight of the baby in my arms, the gentle suck-ling noises as she devoured the bottled breast milk, and the soft leather couch cocooning me as I watched her—something about it all felt right. Then, she pushed the bottle out of her mouth with her tongue, batted her big blue eyes at me, and promptly spit up sour milk all over my favorite purple button down shirt.

Chapter Five

KINSEY

Ring! Ring!

"Hello?" I sniffed, dabbed my nose on a tissue and added it to the many crumpled white balls strewn around me. Reaching for a clean one I heard my on-again, off-again, boyfriend.

"Hey, Kinsey, it's Jason." His jovial voice hurt my ears. Bigger than life, Jason was always ready for a party; it was one of the things I loved about him. "I was wondering if you wanted to head out to the clubs with us?"

"I really feel like staying in tonight, Jason. Could you come over? I had a bad day. I got in a huge fight with my dad." I was in no shape to socialize. I just wanted to wallow in misery on the couch and have someone hold me. My thoughts drifted back to the dog I'd rescued. *I wonder if he's okay?*

"Sorry, Kins," he said. "A bunch of my buddies are heading out to that new club in Times Square. There should be like six or seven of us going." His voice bounced around in my head, adding to my budding migraine. "I don't think I'll make it over to your place. It'll be pretty late by the time we get back from the club."

I sighed. I really didn't want to get all dressed up and go rub elbows with strangers all night. I'd rather call the twenty-four hour vet clinic and check on the pup. Still, I couldn't bring myself to say no. "Sure, okay. When are you going?" I asked, dabbing my eyes with yet another tissue. "It'll take me about 45 minutes to get ready."

Brusquely cutting me off, he continued on. "Hey Kinsey, I'll see you when you get there. I got somebody calling on the other line." He hung up.

It felt like a slap in the face, severing the only human connection I had to provide me any comfort. Never the most emotionally supportive person, I thought Jason might've sensed how upset I was. I'd imagined he'd have shared his sympathy. Maybe when I saw him in person he would.

Standing up, I let the quilt fall back in a heap on my couch and rubbed my face. I really needed a hug, and if I had to go to a club to get one, I guess I would.

Tottering down the sidewalk in my clubbing heels, I pulled on the hem of my short skirt and cursed my horrible luck. It was too cold to be outside walking, and who wants to take the subway to go clubbing? Luckily, my apartment was fairly close to a subway line, but I was still a long way outside the center of the city.

I really wasn't in a partying mood. *Why did I let Jason talk me into going out?*

Looking at my watch, I cursed some more. I would have to change lines twice to get to the right area of Manhattan, and then walk another six blocks to the club. My feet ached more just thinking about it.

Carefully walking down the steps and through the turnstile

into the station, the smooth sounds of jazz drifted over me. A grizzled, stooped old man played a beat up saxophone in the tunnel. His ebony skin was a stark contrast to the short white hairs curling close to his head. Eyes closed, he played his heart out to an audience of harried businessmen rushing home to dinner, co-eds like me drifting by on their way to a night out, and the rats and pigeons that called the tunnel their home.

His battered saxophone case sat at his feet, surrounded by fast food wrappers, cigarette butts, and coffee cups. He gave us a concert worthy of the best jazz club in New York City. I dug into my tiny clutch and pulled out two crumbled one dollar bills. I didn't have much cash, but of what I had, he deserved a share. Had I not already cried my eyes out, his music was so soulful it would have brought me to tears with its haunting melody.

My feet hurt again by the time I got to the bar. Waiting in line behind the velvet rope, I paid my cover charge—yet another $20 gone. I was really going to have to pay attention to how much I was spending. I had no clue how to budget, and I was going to have to pay Dad back. Even the job Mason had offered would take awhile to cover Jason's credit card bills.

The blaring music beat a steady rhythm in my brain. Scanning the room, the dim lighting and psychedelic flashes increased the throbbing tension headache behind my eyes. I rubbed my temples as I scanned the room. *Where's Jason?*

I finally spotted him out on the dance floor, bumping and grinding on some woman in a barely-there neon blue mini skirt. Narrowing my eyes on them, I danced my way out onto the floor and cut in. *Why am I jealous? We're not even serious.* Nevertheless, I couldn't stand the sight of him so close to another woman.

"Hey, Kinsey! You made it!" Jason continued to dance, grinding against me without breaking rhythm.

I swung my hips and let the music take over. The rhythm poured through me, and I sweat the stress away. My headache receded into the background as we wove and twisted through the crowd on the dance floor.

The dancing was therapeutic, but it wasn't solving my problems. When the music switched to a slower song, my emotions started bubbling up again, and I wanted a shoulder to cry on. "Hey, can we find a table?" I shouted at Jason over the blaring music.

"I'm not tired. You go on." He started to dance away, looking for another partner.

"No really, Jason. Let's get a beer or something." I danced after him and grabbed his arm, turning him to face me.

"Fine." He reluctantly left the dance floor and followed me to a quiet corner table. Signaling a waitress, Jason grabbed us two beers and gestured at me. "You got this, right?" He looked at the waitress and pointed at me.

With a sigh, I pulled out twenty dollars and paid the waitress, then I turned myself back to him. "Jason, I really need to talk to you."

"Hey look! There's that girl I was dancing with! Hey, let's ask her to join us!"

"Jason!" I shouted.

He looked at me. "Hey, Kins, it's all cool. Just relax. We're out here to have fun, not to be all serious."

"But Jason, this is serious. I have a real problem!"

"Kinsey, you and me? We have fun." He pointed at me. "You need to relax, or we aren't going to work." Then he paused and seemed to think about it. "You know what? I don't need this stress in my life." And with that, he walked away, leaving me sitting alone at the table. Working the crowd and drinking the beer I'd paid for, he danced his way across the floor just like he danced his way through life—untouched by trouble.

I sat for a minute at the high top bar table, my beer untouched as condensation ran down the side of the cold bottle and pooled around the base. Leaning forward, elbows resting on the sticky table, I held my head in my hands and tried to figure out what I was doing—both there in the club with Jason and in my whole life.

Sitting up and smoothing back the hair falling in my face, I searched the crowd for Jason. Sure enough, I found him back dancing with the girl from earlier. I came to my feet, determined to break them up and try to talk to him again, but then I stopped. I realized there was nothing left to say.

Jason was fun, but we hadn't been serious. I was looking for something. I needed emotional support, a port in the storm to help me weather the fight with my dad, but that wasn't who Jason was. It wasn't what we had ever been. He was done. I guess I was too.

I don't need this.

I turned and left the club without even telling Jason goodbye. Too exhausted to cry, I was going home to sleep. I stopped a moment to dial to the vet clinic. Getting a report on the dog should make me feel better. Hopefully things would look brighter in the morning when I started my new job with Mason. Maybe.

Chapter Six

KINSEY

$\mathcal{M}$y head buzzed with too much caffeine as I surreptitiously wiped my sweaty palms on my skirt, hoping no one would notice. *I knew I shouldn't have had that extra cup of coffee!* In my Manolo Blahnik heels and narrow pencil skirt, I felt like an imposter, a child playing dress up. Only, this wasn't a game. This job was too important to me; I couldn't be my usual klutzy, screwed-up self.

Running into Mason had been a godsend. Walking forward, I straightened my spine and hardened my resolve. I was going to make this work. I could scale the hardest route at the climbing gym and barely break a sweat, but the first day on the job? Even with my determined spirit, I was terrified.

Walking up to the security desk, I bravely smiled at the guard. "Hi. I'm Kinsey Hendrix. I'm here to see Mr. Alexander regarding the executive assistant position."

"Good morning, Miss." He leaned forward a bit, scrutinizing me over the top of his wire-rimmed glasses before looking down at his notes. "Take the third elevator on the left up to the 16th floor. Someone will meet you there." With a brief smile, he unlocked the elevator and I was on my way. I stepped in and as the doors shut, I heard him say, "And welcome to Alexander Tech Enterprises."

Here goes nothing.

On my ride up to the 16th floor, my mind wandered from fear to excitement again. I let myself relax for a moment and my inner teenager began to squeal. *I still can't believe I'm going to be seeing Mason every day!* I felt 14 again, drooling over my teen crush as I pictured his handsome face, his lean six-foot-four-inch frame and dark hair that curled seductively at the collar.

DING!

The sound brought me back to reality as the elevator doors slid open. A beautiful, silver-haired woman stood waiting for me. I tamped down my enthusiasm and tried my best to appear professional.

"Miss Hendrix?" Her smile wrapped around me like a warm blanket. I instantly started to relax under her gaze.

"Yes. I'm Kinsey Hendrix." I held out my hand in greeting.

She grasped it in hers. "So lovely to meet you. I'm Mary Stewart, Mr. Alexander's executive assistant." Her voice was melodic; it reminded me of my grandmother's. "I have a few things for you to sign, and then we'll get right to it."

"Thank you, Ms. Stewart." I loved this woman already. She was motherly and professional all at the same time. I wanted to be just like her.

"Mary, please," she told me. "We are going to be working closely today." She started down the hall at a brisk pace, her heels tapping a jaunty rhythm as I struggled to keep up with her. "I have a lot to teach you and very little time. My mother gets out of the hospital tomorrow, and I need to be there to take her home." I followed her down the brightly lit hallway, past several large glass-fronted offices, to the big office at the very end. Spanning the entire width of the building, it held a smaller desk in front of an entryway, and then a larger one in a big room behind.

Mary stopped at the first desk and gestured for me to have a seat. I did. She pulled up a second chair. "This is my desk. Now it's yours, too."

~

B *ZZZZ..... BZZZZZ.....*
   "Kinsey, Mr. Alexander is paging you." Mary patiently pointed at yet another flashing light on the phone. I poked at it, but nothing happened. "No. Like this." Effortlessly, she made the buzzing stop and asked him what he needed.

When she was done, she put the phone down and turned her attention back to me. "Ok. Next time press here," she pointed to a button on the top of the phone, "and here," another button, "and pick up the handset." Thank God she was patient with me. "Now he wants coffee. You remember where everything is?"

I nodded confidently. "Yes. I can do that. I can make coffee." Who was I kidding? At that point, I was so overwhelmed I probably couldn't even have spelled my own name. "He prefers it black, right?" I asked, my voice trembling.

"Yes. You *can* do this, Kinsey." Her hand covered mine, stilling the nervous tapping of my fingers on the paper desk pad.

Almost in a daze, I rose from the desk and made my way to Mason's personal coffee maker. It was the fanciest espresso machine I'd ever seen. With a built-in grinder, double boilers, and more spouts than I knew what to do with, each cup was made to order.

My shoulders sank at the sight of it. Even a cup of coffee was beyond my skill set. Then Mary, like an angel, guided me step-by-step through the process.

A few minutes later, I tottered into Mason's office, cautiously balancing his coffee cup so I wouldn't spill a drop. The last thing I needed was for my klutziness to rear its ugly head. A vision of splashing hot coffee all over my gorgeous new boss flashed before my eyes and gave me chills.

As I carefully slid the cup and saucer onto his gleaming glass and steel desk, my fingers accidentally brushed his. The sensation sent tingles up my arm that pushed away all my fear. I could just imagine those fingers dancing over my skin. I felt the warmth of his gaze as he turned his steel blue eyes in my direction. Heat rose from the swell of my breasts up to the roots of my hair, and I couldn't help but blush.

Mason held me trapped by his stare. I couldn't move. I could feel the blood circulating through my body, my heartbeat accelerating. He smelled amazing, his scent subtle, masculine, and magnetic. I wanted desperately to get closer.

Ding!

"Thank you, Kinsey. That will be all." Distracted by the beeping of his cell phone, he quickly shifted his gaze away. Maybe I was overreacting, imagining things. I sure thought that was desire I'd just seen in his eyes, but as quickly as it turned me on, he turned it off.

A few hours later, my head spun with information overload. It was time to go home, but I had so much left to do. Mary was a hard taskmaster. I could now recite the entire company structure, operate a space station level phone system, and formulate Mason's current schedule for the next six months. I was proud of what I'd accomplished, and I wanted to achieve even more.

The work consumed me, and I jumped at the sound of a voice interrupting my train of thought. "You're not ready to quit on me, are you?" Mason stood tall and handsome, watching me from his office door. I could feel myself flushing yet again under his eye.

I fought to cool the heat building inside me. "No. Mary

has been wonderful. She left a few minutes ago. I was just getting a few things ready for tomorrow morning."

He walked toward my desk, a wolfish gleam in his eye. I felt his nearness as he stood over me, smelled his masculine scent. My mouth went dry, and I could feel my blood pulsing through me. I held my breath in anticipation.

Leaning forward, he cupped my face in his large hand and gazed into my eyes. Tiny electric charges zipped through my body from his touch. Melting back into the black leather office chair, my lips parted and my breath escaped as barely a whisper. "Yes?"

He grinned. "When's my first meeting?"

I blinked. *What? Meeting? OH!* "Ah, um, yes," I stammered. "Your first meeting is at eight-thirty with the head of your gaming division. At ten-thirty, you meet the finance office. And at noon, you have lunch with a member of the board." The words came tumbling out in a rush. His nearness rattled me. I couldn't think with him so close, but close was where I wanted him.

He stood up, shifting away from me. "Thank you Miss Hendrix. I will see you tomorrow at eight o'clock sharp." And then he was gone, moving silently like a jungle cat. His power and magnetism followed him, leaving the room empty and me bereft.

Chapter Seven

MASON

I wiped a film of sweat from my forehead. Working with her was magic, but when the work day ended and she left, it was torture to be without her.

Just the thought of Kinsey's scent—jasmine, it must have been—made my throat constrict. I cleared it and tried to catch my breath. In the office, my body's reaction to her nearness was beyond my control. I was almost relieved whenever my phone rang or a crisis called for my attention. It put some space between us. I needed and dreaded that space.

At home, the space killed me. I sat staring at my cell phone, tapping my pen nervously, my leg jiggling. *Where's my usual cool, calm self?* I wanted to call Kinsey. I wanted to hear how her day was. Screw that, I just wanted to hear her voice. *What is happening to me?*

Mark teased me mercilessly that I would never settle down. He loved to hear about my escapades and always called when he saw me in photos online with yet another woman. Being featured in People's Sexiest Men edition last year had been great for my sex life, but not so helpful for forming any type of emotional attachment to a woman. I never knew when I met someone if they wanted me for me or wanted me for the man in the magazine. I never had any trouble getting my needs met. It came so easily sex had grown rather boring.

Of course, Mark laughed when I complained. Married for five years with six-month-old twins, his sex life was non-existent. His wife, exhausted by the constant nursing and lack of sleep, was a hard no in that department. She was also adamant that Mark would help and that their kids wouldn't be raised by a nannies and babysitters like Mark and I were. Well, like we were until Dad died. Anyway, all that work meant that he wasn't getting any, and he envied my unlimited supply. He didn't realize how quickly it grew old.

The women I met were all smoking hot, and they would all do anything I asked. I was bored out of my skull with the beauty queen buffet. Kinsey was a different kind of delicious. She was unique. She wanted more—a degree, a profession, a life of her own, not just a seat next to a rich husband at society dinner parties. She wanted more than just… *me.*

Kinsey changed the game on me. There I was, as nervous as a teenager about to call his first crush. Instead of dodging phone calls, I was searching for the courage to pick up the phone and call her. *What am I doing?*

I only lasted a few nights before I just couldn't take it anymore. I missed her when she wasn't near. I wanted to be with her.

Fumbling to pick up my phone, I dropped my pen and watched as it rolled across the glass top of my desk and fell to the plush cream carpet. Bending down to retrieve it, I bumped my head on the underside of my desk. Cursing, I rubbed the spot. *What is wrong with me?‽?!!!*

The anxiety made me angry, which gave me enough courage to pick up the phone. I was going to call Kinsey. She was going to prove to be just like every other woman—pretty on the outside, empty on inside. I was going to see her for who she really was and get this fascination out of my system once and for all. I stabbed the call button with my finger and listened as it rang.

"Hello?" Kinsey's melodic voice answered on the first ring.

"Ah… hi. Um… it's me, Mason."

"Oh, Mason! Sorry. I didn't recognize the number."

"I apologize for calling so late, but I… um…" I scrambled to come up with a good excuse for calling. I should have thought of that before I'd dialed. A thousand ideas came to me at once, but only one would bring me closer to her.

"Mason?"

I cleared my throat. "I just uh, wanted to say you did a good job today." I stammered and stuttered my way through.

"Sorry," she said. "You caught me in the middle of studying for my last final." I pictured her with her hair in a messy bun, one pen stuck in the back of it, chewing on the end of another as she made notes in the margins of her text-book. "What's up? You need me to do something?"

"Ah, no, sorry for interrupting you. I'll see you in the morning."

Silence stretched across the phone lines. I could hear Kinsey breathing, but she wasn't saying anything. Had I blown it? I really just wanted an excuse to hear her voice.

"Oh, ok. I'll see you tomorrow."

"Wait… Kinsey?"

"Yes?"

"Will you go to lunch with me tomorrow?"

"Um, sure."

"Ok, twelve o'clock, I'll have the limo pick us up."

"Um, ok, sounds good. Goodnight Mason."

"'Night, Kins." I leaned back. I was doomed if just hearing her voice was all it took to put a smile on my face.

Chapter Eight

MASON

This was a bad idea. Stupid. She's gonna see right through me.

What had felt like a great idea when I'd asked her to lunch, suddenly felt like a pathetic trick to win over a pretty girl. I hadn't been this nervous about a girl since I was fourteen and asked Cindy Johnson to homecoming. Of course, back then I was a freshman, barely five-foot-five, had braces and acne, and my voice still squeaked. The summer between freshman and sophomore year, I matured and my life changed. By senior year, I was six-foot-four and starting receiver for my high school football team. I'd never felt nervous again... until Kinsey.

With her, all those insecurities came rushing back. I never should have offered her the job. I didn't know how I was going to work with her every day, seeing her sitting at that desk. She made me feel like a teenager just discovering my first crush.

I shook my head; I had to focus. She was all woman, with her long legs, taut physique, and a smile that could bring a man to his knees. My body's response to her was beyond my control.

I moved swiftly down the hall, into the elevator, and down to the lobby. If I didn't know better, I would have thought I was running away. Over the years, I had successfully avoided the entanglements of relationships. Work had always been my sanctuary. By hiring Kinsey, I'd made it my own personal torture chamber.

~

A waiter led us to a table for two by the big front windows. Our table overlooked the busy street, and I could see business women out for lunch, society women walking by with shopping bags, men with briefcases, joggers, and kids with their nannies.

Moments later, another waiter in a starched white shirt and maroon vest approached us. "Welcome to the Bistro. My name is Andrew and I'll be serving you today. What can I get you to drink?"

I nodded in Kinsey's direction. "The lady would like…?"

"A sour apple martini with Grey Goose." Alcohol might not be the answer to everything, but Kinsey sure looked like she needed a drink right then.

I nodded. "I'll have a scotch on the rocks."

"I was surprised last night when you called and asked me to lunch." She leaned back in her chair and closed her eyes for a moment. "I'm sorry I wasn't more talkative, studying for finals has been hell."

I stayed silent and watched her as we waited for our drinks. My eyes roamed her perfect nose, her sun-kissed cheeks, and waves of fair hair. She was a beautiful woman.

The waiter returned and set our glasses in front of us. Beads of condensation ran down the outside of the glasses and soaked into the white tablecloth.

I reached across the table and tilted her head up. "The dark circles aren't too noticeable, I remember finals, I don't envy you the long hours hitting the books after working for me."

Just one finger touching her chin sent jolts of electricity through my body. *Why am I reacting this way?*

Kinsey shook her head and squared her shoulders. She lifted her chin to look me straight in the eye. "I'll be okay. It's almost over."

I listened to her talk about her classes as I sat across from her in the bustling cafe.

"Do you remember when I first started coming to dinner with my brother?" I asked Kinsey when we hit a lull in the conversation.

"I think your brother started coming over first, right?" She grew pensive as she thought back to those years. "And then you started tagging along after a few months?"

"Yes. Mom was working all the time, always at her two jobs, and I was a wild teenager up to no good. Mark first brought me with him to keep me out of trouble. Then later, I asked to come so I could learn more about the business."

Kinsey shook her head. "Dad was so proud of you two. First, your brother when he started learning his business, then, how quickly you picked up on everything he told you. I was so jealous."

"Those meals were great! I learned so much from your dad. I couldn't have asked for a better mentor. Noah is an amazing businessman."

"He is," she said flatly, her eyes narrowing, obviously still angry from their last encounter.

I decided to change the subject back to school. "How are your other classes going?

"I'm on the Dean's List." Kinsey was quick to answer.

I wasn't surprised she was doing well in school. Kinsey had always possessed a great mind, reading the science section of the New York Times religiously after those dinners, trying not to look like she was listening to our shoptalk.

"That is wonderful, congratulations."

"When will Mary be back? Finals are in a week or so, and then I have the summer off, but I have one more year."

"Mary will hopefully be back before fall classes start. Don't worry about it, we'll work it out." Andrew showed up with bread and salads. "We'll go over work stuff tomorrow. For now, we eat."

KINSEY

I *s this a mistake? Will working for Mason anger my father?* Studying him across the table, Mason could have modeled for Calvin Klein. He was that hot. His square jaw, shadowed by a layer of stubble, reminded me of the lead singer of a rock band. His looks had matured since he was a teenager. His features were sharper, and he had a few gray strands peeking out from a full head of thick black hair. From what I had felt when he'd steadied me at the elevator, under his designer suit was a sculpted physique even better than the one I'd admired in his twenties.

Mason exuded a subtle power. As a teen he was a dashing, bright young man. As an accomplished businessman, a compelling presence radiated from him. He looked at me with an intensity and confidence that I found myself helplessly drawn to.

Sitting at the cafe table, peering at Mason over my martini glass, I closed my eyes. I could still feel those powerful muscles rippling under my finger. Stumbling and landing in the arms of the stranger who tried to run me over on his way out of the elevator had been a stroke of delicious luck.

As we dined, he asked questions. We chatted about school, the dog I couldn't stop thing about. In my mind I named her P.J. He seemed so interested in me. My thoughts betrayed me and I kept thinking of how he'd held me that morning with his strong hands. His long fingers would have been perfect for playing a grand piano... or a woman. I admired how he moved as if he owned every room he entered, was aware of everyone and everything around us.

T he limo pulled up to the curb in front of the office, and came to a gentle stop. I watched through the tinted window as the doorman came out of the building and stood by the door, ready to open it when we emerged.

"Kinsey," he started. Maybe it was the drink, but hearing my name on his lips, the sound coming it out in one slow moan, pushed me past the limits of discretion.

At first, I just leaned forward to give him a quick peck on the cheek as thanks for a wonderful lunch. But then, when his eyes widened and he froze, I lost it. My breath caught and I moved to sit back. His hands reached forward and I found myself unable to move. Strong hands pulled me back in and our lips met... the kiss so gentle, I barely felt it.

As if outside myself, I watched as I moved. Even while I told myself to stop, I made the next move and slid over the leather seat, climbing into his lap.

He seemed startled, his pupils dilating and his nostrils flaring, but then he gathered me in his arms, pulled me closer, and lowered his head. I tilted my head back to meet him as his lips brushed mine. I melted into his arms, and he kissed me again. The hunger on his lips filled me with need. I whimpered, my arms wrapping around him as I tried to climb inside his skin. I had dreamt of this moment for years, and it was so much better than I'd imagined.

He cradled my head as his lips met mine for a third time, and I could feel his member swelling as he pulled me closer. He laid feather-soft kisses on my eyelids and nose, but then he hesitated as if arguing with himself. Finally he pressed his mouth to mine again.

I didn't want it to end, but he suddenly set me back down on the seat, out of breath, grimacing as he adjusted himself in his pants.

I lifted a hand to my lips, where I could still feel the lingering echo of his kiss against my trembling fingers. A sudden awkwardness rose between us.

The intercom broke the mood, the driver's voice crackling into the super heated space.

"Mr. Alexander, we are here."

We exchanged glances, and I took a deep breath. Before I could say anything, the door opened and the doorman reached in to help me out.

What have I done?

Chapter Nine

KINSEY

$\mathcal{A}$ door slammed somewhere down the hall, and the sound bounced off the walls and echoed through the glass and steel offices. Sitting in my comfy ergonomic chair, I jumped as my hand flew to my chest. I was staying late to tidy up some last minute details. I wanted to finish up my first week filling in for Mary without any mistakes. I'd thought I was alone.

Looking up from the computer screen, I blinked owlishly, my eyes taking a minute to adjust to the dusky gloom of the quiet offices. Peering through the glass walls I spotted Mason striding down the hall towards me from the elevators. My breath hitched as I took him in. He was magnificent even in a sweat-soaked t-shirt and jogging shorts.

He must have just come from his private gym two floors down. Entries in his calendar blocked out two hours every weekday for workout time, either early morning or late evening. Admiring him as he came closer, I could see his muscles rippling under the tight workout clothes. His biceps strained against his shirt sleeves, and the thin cotton outlined his broad chest perfectly. He really was a magnificent male specimen. My heart skipped a beat remembering the kiss in the limo earlier in the week.

"What are you still doing here, Kinsey?" He asked me, toweling off his hair as he walked by my desk without even looking at me.

I frowned, but he didn't see it. "I wanted to figure out how to sync my calendar to yours so all the appointments transfer over." Turning to follow him with my eyes, I told myself he was my boss—*only* my boss. I had to keep reminding myself of that.

I was still having trouble with a few programs on the computer, but I didn't want Mason to think he'd made a mistake hiring me. We hadn't spoken since we'd ended our lunch with that amazing kiss and then hadn't spoken of it since.

Tossing his sweaty towel over a chair, Mason went to stand behind his desk. He muttered something as he rummaged through his files, but my attention was caught by the messy black hair standing up on one side in wet spikes. *I wonder what it would feel like to run my fingers through it.* I had gone to sleep every night replaying our kiss, and woke up every morning with a smile.

I had to mentally shake myself to escape that fantasy before he caught me staring. "Can I help you with something?" I asked.

"I'm looking for the Mao Fang file," Mason mumbled, still digging through the stacks. "There's a problem with the factory in China."

"I have it right here." I straightened my skirt, walked over to his mailbox, and fished the thick manila folder out of the jumble piled inside. "Mr. Lu Feng's secretary called this morning to schedule a phone call with accounting."

As I pivoted on one 3 inch heel, I found myself teetering. The heel snapped free of the sole, and I stumbled. Before I could fall, Mason reacted, reaching out with his strong hand to grab my arm and steady me.

"Thanks," I whispered, mortified that he'd had to rescue me yet again.

He stared as he held me until he was sure I was okay. Then he reached over to grab the file I was still clutching. Again, forgetting why we should stay apart, I reveled in his nearness; even his sweaty musk was attractive.

The disappointment crushed me when he walked away without even glancing back at me. "Thanks for finding that," he called back over his shoulder.

I was sure he wanted me. The kiss in the limo the other day wasn't a fluke. He was as hungry for it as I was, but he hadn't made a move since. That kiss had been amazing, but I was starting to worry I'd made too much out of it.

The more I got to know Mason, the more I realized we had in common, and the more attracted to him I became. But maybe he wasn't attracted to me. Self-doubt flooded my mind. *Why would he pick klutzy, messed up me when he could have any woman he wanted?*

As insecurity bombarded me, he stopped and turned back. "Can you come in to my office for a moment?" he asked.

"Um, sure." I stuttered. Frightened, I thought of all the work I'd done over the last week. *Did I mess something up?*

Mason turned and walked into his office. I stood there, taking a moment to wipe my sweaty hands on my skirt and straighten my hair. I needed to pull myself together before following him. With a deep breath, I limped down the hall on my one good heel. When I reached the open door, I stopped and gaped at him.

In the center of his glass desk, a lovely carved chess board was set up and waiting for players. My heart sang. *He remembered!*

"Care for a game?" he asked with a smile, as he settled into his leather office chair.

"Ah… sure. You still play?" I asked, as he crooked an eyebrow at me, a playful gleam in his eye. I took that as a yes and hobbled over to the seat opposite him.

"I don't play as often as I used to," he said. "As I recall, you were quite the strategist as a teen. I thought maybe this might be fun." He pulled his chair up to his desk and steepled his fingers. "Your move."

Chapter Ten

MASON

*L*eaning against the shower wall, hot water streaming down my back, I groaned as I replayed my dream from the night before. When I'd woken up, it had taken me a minute to realize Kinsey was not in bed with me, that it had all been a dream. A hot, wet, sweaty dream that left me aching for her.

Reaching down, I took myself in my hand. I was going to have to deal with my need; otherwise, I wouldn't be able to concentrate at work. Not with her so close.

Slick with soap, my engorged cock filled my hand. I stroked slowly at first and then faster and faster, imagining the warm wetness was Kinsey. I could almost see her big blue eyes looking up at me, her golden hair spread across the pillow. I wanted to feel myself buried deep inside her as she clenched around me. The fantasy swallowed me, and I didn't last long.

"Ooooooooh!" I moaned long and loud. Coming in hot spurts, I shot jets of thick cum against the shower wall. Turning, I collapsed against the tiles, water dripping off my nose as I caught my breath. *What the hell am I going to do about Kinsey?*

Since I'd first bumped into her at Noah's office, she'd dominated my every thought. I couldn't escape her awake or asleep. She was all around me, and when she wasn't, she was inside my head.

I shouldn't have kissed her the other day. That kiss had only made things ten times worse. I couldn't even look at her anymore. All I wanted to do was pull her up against me and bury myself in her. *I should be focusing on the China disaster! Those problems aren't going to solve themselves!*

Unfortunately, my head was filled with nothing but visions of Kinsey. I hadn't wanted to let go that day. I had wanted to pull her closer, but instead I'd released her and walked away. At least, I'd tried to.

∼

I collapsed into my office chair. *What am I going to do about China?*

"Kinsey, will you please pull any emails from the finance department concerning the Mao Fang electronics factory?" I asked over the office intercom as I flipped through the file. I hoped she could find something. If production of our graphics card stopped, we couldn't provide the part needed to play our best-selling game. No one wanted to play a game that constantly pixelated or buffered. It would be a disaster for our gaming division, which brought in 85% of our revenue.

"Anything else? I'm just about done here." Kinsey swept in, the air filling with the subtle jasmine fragrance of her perfume. My mind temporarily short-circuited as I hid my reaction to her presence behind my desk. That kiss was going to haunt me forever.

"Not unless you know how to get the Chinese to lift the order shutting down our factory." I reached for the emails she held out and started to skim through them. "We finally got the factory running again after everyone caught that flu, running around the clock trying to fill orders, and then the government decided that since we were paying above minimum wage to the workers, and we could afford to pay everyone while they were off, we must have enough to pay more taxes. They're asking four times what we pay now."

Pulling a chair up to my desk, Kinsey sat down. "Who is your contact in the labor department?"

Startled by her question, I stared for a moment before I could answer. "Lu Fan is our overseer in the Department of Labor," I finally said. Stopping for a moment, I thought about how much to tell her. "I am supposed to meet with the US Ambassador to China tomorrow, but I don't know if I can get everything ready in time to fly to Beijing in the morning."

"Ambassador Williams?" Kinsey asked excitedly, suddenly looking very pleased with herself.

"Uh, yes. We've only talked over the phone, but he's going with me to meet Lu Fan." I felt like I should know more than I did. *Why did she look so happy?*

"Wonderful! What do you have put together? He's going to want a copy of everything."

Why did I feel like she knew more than I did? It was a rather unsettling feeling for me. "I've got the financial stuff from my meeting today and these emails, but I'm going to be here all night putting the presentations together since Mary is gone." I eyed her curiously. "Do you know the Ambassador?"

"Of course! He's great friends with Dad! He comes over for dinner every time he's in town. His son Hugh is here at the university in one of my chemistry classes, too." Kinsey acted like it was normal to dine with foreign dignitaries all the time. I guess for a Hendrix, it was. She continued, "Give me the data. I can put together your presentation packets."

I held up what I had, and Kinsey took it and started back to her office. I stared after her. *Who is this woman?*

"Kinsey?" I called after her. An idea was forming. I was either brilliant or insane. "Would you like to go with me?"

R ubbing the sleep from my eyes, I peered at the clock on my computer. It was just past six in the morning. We were finally done with just enough time to head to the airport.

China was 12 hours behind us, so we would arrive early in the morning, right before all the government offices opened. Standing up and stretching, I gathered up the files and stuffed them haphazardly into my leather briefcase. Looking around for Kinsey, I found her asleep at her desk.

"Kinsey?" Bending over her, I gently shook her shoulder to wake her up. "Kinsey? It's time to go."

Her blonde hair had fallen loose from the tight bun she wore at work to keep the long strands contained. They flowed across her desk and spilled over the edge in a golden waterfall "Wha?" Blearily, she raised her head, blinked her eyes, and stared at me with a vacant expression.

I was caught like a deer in the headlights, trapped in her sleepy gaze. Even waking up, her head pillowed on her arms, sitting at her desk in yesterday's wrinkled clothes, she was beautiful. There were creases on her face and ink smudges on her cheek. It had been a long, busy night and she had been a trouper. She had more than exceeded any expectations I'd had. A fully-trained temp from an executive agency couldn't have done better. It really was amazing how my spur-of-the-moment offer of employment had worked out so well.

"We have to go, Kins," I said gently, "our flight leaves in a little over an hour."

"What?" She asked, her brain finally kicking into gear. "I fell asleep! I haven't packed! I'm not ready! Did you finish the last report?" Her eyes darted back-and-forth frantically.

"Calm down. We have just enough time to swing by your apartment for a few things. We've just got to hurry."

"Then let's go. What do I need to take?" She jumped up,

grabbed her high heels from the floor and her purse from the chair. "I'm ready."

Standing there, barefoot, her golden hair wild around her shoulders, the sun shined behind her like a golden halo. A button had come undone on her blouse, and her skirt had risen above her knees. She looked like a warrior, fierce and determined. This was a side of Kinsey I had never seen before.

I loved it.

KINSEY

Waking up to Mason was just as wonderful as I thought it would be. Only, I had never pictured myself with messy hair, drooling, and wearing last night's crumpled clothes... in the office. *Oh My God! I need to brush my teeth!* I could smell my own dragon breath.

Yawning and stretching, I stood and gathered my things. I wondered, *do we have time to stop for coffee?* I'm not sure I could survive a long overseas plane ride on half a soda and some peanuts while squished into a tin can with 300 of my closest friends. *Will Mason spring for first class?*

"Ok. I'm ready." I walked out of the office to the elevator with purse slung over my shoulder. I finger brushed my hair in an effort to look presentable.

"Let's go," he said. "You've got ten minutes to pack when we get to your apartment." All business, Mason was in executive mode, single-mindedly focused on getting us to the airport and prepping for his meeting.

We quickly left the building, and I reveled in the plush limo seats, wishing I could catch another quick nap. Unfortunately, the trip to my apartment was too short.

"Ten minutes," Mason reminded me as we climbed the stairs to my second floor entrance. I was thrilled with the open spaces and great views from my apartment, but the building was old. It had to be antique to occupy such prime downtown real-estate, but that meant the elevators were iffy and there was no central air. That day was a no-elevator day.

Wiping the beads of sweat from my upper lip, I unlocked the door to my apartment and sighed as the first blast of cool air from the window unit hit me and soothed my flushed cheeks.

"Have a seat," I told him. "I'll be done in just a minute." I gestured to my white, overstuffed couch, which sat in front of the AC unit in the living room.

In a rush, I started stripping before I was even out of the room, dropping my blouse and skirt in the bedroom as I continued walking straight to the bathroom. I figured I had two minutes to shower and eight to pack. I beat my time, and was standing in front of Mason, squeaky clean with a packed roller suitcase and a small carry-on bad in eight and a half minutes.

"Let's go." I said gazing down at Mason. He had fallen asleep on my couch, head resting on my starfish pillow with my grandma's crocheted throw across his legs.

For just a moment, when first waking, Mason looked up at me with desire. I basked in the glow, but it only lasted for a moment. As he became more alert, the shutters fell over his eyes, and his lust seemed to vanish. The business man I knew was back.

"Let me carry that for you," Mason said as he escorted me down to the waiting limo.

We rode in silence the full hour to the airport. I was prepared to dash across the terminal in a race to beat departure time, but instead of heading to the regular check-in and security, we stopped in front of a different door.

"Right this way, sir." A man in a pilot's uniform was waiting, and led us down a hallway, handing our passports to the woman behind an unlabeled check-in desk. I was really confused at this point.

"Have a lovely flight, sir," she said with a smile. It only took her a moment to scan our passports and hand them back. Then the pilot led us out glass double doors, and my jaw dropped.

Oh my God! We're flying in his private jet!!!

Chapter Eleven

KINSEY

I gasped as we walked up the steps and into a spacious interior. My eyes took in the plush leather reclining seats, a full-sized dinner table, and down the hall, I spotted an entire bedroom through a narrow doorway.

"Welcome." A woman appeared out of nowhere. "If you will both come this way, breakfast is almost ready." The way-too-perky stewardess led us to a beautifully-set table with a white table-cloth, shiny silver flatware, and crystal juice glasses. I sat opposite Mason, and after placing the cloth napkin in my lap, the stewardess—I think she said her name was Marie—poured us each a glass of water before she went off in search of coffee.

"Mason, I had no idea." I looked around with wide eyes, afraid to touch anything.

"What did you expect, Kinsey? How else can I have a business meeting in the US in the morning and be in China in time for a dinner meeting?" Mason chuckled as he leaned back and took a sip of the steaming brew that magically appeared before us. "This plane is a tool just like any other I use to do business."

Sipping my coffee after a liberal application of cream and sugar, I sighed with gusto as the hot liquid hit my stomach and the heat spread to my chilly limbs. I guess private jets were cold just like commercial planes.

"That makes sense, but Dad always flew us first class. He said private jets were too expensive to maintain."

"I time-share with two other executives. Luckily, we rarely need her at the same time. I find it worth the boost in productivity. I can't be in two places at once, but this helps. Plus, I'm well-rested, well-fed, and I can work on the way. Even in first class, I can't spread out and problem solve like I need too. Besides," his eyes began to smolder, "I get to be alone with you."

Blushing, I hid behind my coffee cup as my eyes flew back to the bedroom doorway. *Does he mean what I think he does?*

Clearing my throat, I turned and looked out the window. We had almost finished crossing the bottom of Florida and were heading out across the Gulf of Mexico. Before me stretched miles of ocean that were quickly disappearing under a thick layer of clouds as we rapidly ascended to 30,000 feet.

"Thank you," I said, as I turned back to the stewardess who'd brought us a chilled fruit plate and a Spanish omelet. My mouth began to water. *How long has it been since I've eaten?*

"Hungry?" Mason asked as I wolfed down half the omelet in a very unladylike 30 seconds. "I guess we did skip dinner last night." He smiled and picked up his fork. He must have discovered how amazing the food was because he didn't speak for the next few minutes.

"How long is the flight?" I asked, looking out the window again.

"About 15 hours. We cross the gulf, and once we hit Central America, we'll turn slightly north for China. It could be a little shorter if the winds favor us and push us along

faster. She's got a range of over 7,500 miles at Mach 0.8."
Leaning back, he crossed his legs and picked up a newspaper.
"We'll stop and refuel in Tokyo, but that won't take long."

Wow, I really was naive. I thought Dad was pretentious, but
this level of luxury was off the charts.

"Have you always traveled like this?"

"Well," Clearing his throat, he ducked his head, a move
that made him look like a vulnerable little boy for a moment.
"No. Growing up, we didn't have much."

Raising an eyebrow, I didn't say anything but waited to see
if he would share anything else. I wasn't going to miss this
opportunity to learn more about Mason.

"Dad died when I was young. Mom had to work a lot.
Traveling like this was a pipe dream."

MASON

Kinsey had looked shell-shocked when we walked out to
the plane. I guess I should have prepared her, but I
figured a private jet would be old hat. Noah must have really
kept her sheltered over the years. No wonder she panicked
when he cut her off.

Breakfast had been great, but what I really wanted was
Kinsey. That kiss in the limo had blown me away. Our attraction was undeniable, and I didn't know what to do about it.

I couldn't believe I'd talked about my childhood. I didn't
tell anybody about that. Mom knew I had donated money to
the shelter, but neither she nor Mark knew I volunteered there.
Kinsey brought things out of me I thought were buried deep.

As she slept, I read through several reports and made
notes for our meeting that evening. Leaning back, I thought
about what to do. There was roughly an 8-year difference in
our ages. Did that matter? She was an adult. I was an adult.
She seemed into me, and I was definitely into her.

I itched to run a finger down her cheek. Her skin looked soft, pink with the flush of sleep. Rather than going into the bedroom, which I knew she was curious about, she had chosen to recline her leather chair and curl up with the soft, fuzzy blanket the stewardess provided. She'd almost immediately fallen asleep.

Tapping my pen on the open file in front of me, I waited for the noise to wake her up. *What am I doing?* Her eyes fluttered open, dreamy and unfocused. She saw me watching her, her big blue eyes locked onto mine, telegraphing her increasing need. I reached over and touched her cheek, my finger running down her neck and along her collar bone. I felt myself hardening. Parting her lips, she gave a little sigh as my finger dipped below the collar of her blouse and caressed the soft flesh of her plump breasts.

Her chest rose as her breath came faster. She slowly leaned forward. Moistening her lips, she spoke. "Mason?" Her breath came out in a rush, whispering my name.

I knew it was wrong. I was too old. She was too young. She worked for me, and what's worse, she my best friend's daughter. Noah trusted me, but God, these last few days together, working with Kinsey, seeing her every day, watching her come alive as she settled into her position at the office—I was afraid I was falling for her.

Dipping my head I leaned forward just enough so my lips brushed hers. The air sizzled at our kiss, and Kinsey melted beneath me.

"We shouldn't. Not yet." The words came out with a sigh as I tried to pull back, my balls aching with the need to bury myself in her warmth. "This is all happening too fast."

Kinsey was not to be denied. "I don't care," she whispered. She reached up and pulled my face toward her again. This time our lips connected with a fierce passion. "I don't care," she said again between kisses. "I need you."

What man could resist that? *Not me.* I wasn't that strong.

"Are you clean?" she whispered in my ear.

I nodded, my eyes flashing. *This is really going to happen!*

"Me too." She nibbled on the soft edge of my ear. "And I'm on the pill."

Suddenly, the alpha male awakened in me. Reason was gone. All my earlier excuses were forgotten. Reaching down, I scooped her up, cradled her against my chest as I strode back to the bedroom, and kicked the door shut behind me. I became the aggressor, taking over the seduction and gently but firmly dropping her on the bed so I could drink in her beauty.

KINSEY

L anding with a bounce on the luxurious bed where Mason dropped me, I reached up, my hands working feverishly to undo all the buttons on his crisp dress shirt. I was dying to expose what was underneath. *Would it be as amazing as I imagined?* Pushing his shirt off his wide shoulders exposed the broad, chiseled chest I had dreamt about.

My hands roamed over the flat plains, tracing the hard muscles, and running through the light dusting of dark hair. I couldn't help myself. I wanted to *feel* more of him. Dragging him down on top of me, I reveled in the heat of his firm, lean body pressed against me. When I pulled him even closer, I could feel his hardness growing. His long rod telegraphed the throbbing need nestled perfectly in the cleft between my legs.

"I want you, Mason," I begged. Growing wetter, I could feel a trickle of moisture running down my inner thigh. I tried to wriggle even closer, hungry to feel him inside me.

My eyes fluttered closed for a moment and I stopped moving. Breathing in his scent, my libido rose fast. My body quivered with unmet need. Suddenly, I felt his weight leave me and a devastating sense of loss filled me. My chest rose and fell with wanton breath as I listened to the clink of his belt and then the light thud of his pants hitting the floor. Peeking for just a moment I took in the sculpted expanse of tanned muscle, the sprinkling of curls on his chest that formed a trail down into the waistband of his black boxer briefs. Then he was above me, his shadow falling across my body and blocking the light.

Delicately, almost reverently, he began to strip my clothes from me. He spread my silky blouse wide and unwrapped me like a precious gift, sitting back on his heels to admire me as I lay there, chest heaving. Then he licked his lips and unhooked the front clasp of my lacy white bra, palmed my breasts gently in his strong hands, and playfully pinched my nipples until they hardened in his fingers. The pleasure of his touch was so intense I barely noticed my skirt and panties sliding over my hips, down my legs, and past my feet to be discarded and forgotten on the floor.

"Are you sure?" He paused for just a moment at the end of the bed.

"Yes!" I breathed out.

The bed dipped with his weight, and suddenly he was hovering above me once again. "You are so beautiful," he whispered. "Your skin is soft like silk." He kissed my breasts. "Your curves are irresistible." He proceeded to explore my body, his muscles quivering with fragile restraint. Below, his manhood swelled and flushed with need. "I want to be inside you."

"Yes, Mason, yes!" Wiggling beneath him, I was mad with lust. "Please, Mason, I want to feel you inside me!"

"I want to bury myself in you." Whispering, he kissed me again as his fingers stroked between my legs. "Right here. I want to feel your slick, wet heat envelop me." I felt his fingers, deep inside me, massaging my g-spot, feeding the flames of my desire. "You're mine," he whispered.

Then he wasn't talking anymore. Instead, he worshipped my body. His hands kneaded and caressed me from shoulders to hips, followed by his gifted lips. The warm wetness of his tongue made me squirm as he took one nipple in his mouth and sucked, and my back arched off the bed. His stubble, rough on my tender skin, sent tingles up and down my nerve endings. Moments later, I felt his other hand gliding down my chest, over my other breast, first tweaking the nipple, fondling my round globe, and then creeping lower and lower toward my center. With one finger, he began gently massaging my clit as his mouth licked and sucked both breasts.

He focused on his work, jaw clenched as he explored me. I could feel his member swelling, and I ached to feel the satin-smooth flesh, to explore it with my hands and mouth, to taste the slightly salty musk on my tongue. His hands were like magic, and I lost my focus, my entire being centered on the growing pressure between my legs.

"Oh, God," I cried out, drowning in pleasure as my orgasm rose, the spiral of sensation coiling tighter and tighter. "Mason!" I screamed as I felt the first wave build. He kept one hand busy, his fingers flicking and rubbing my center. With the other hand, he gently slipped two fingers inside me, curling them up to stroke my spot again. I felt the wave cresting, and then pushing me over the edge as he massaged the walls of my canal while at the same time leaning down and devouring, adoring my clit. Soon, the orgasm rolled over me, wave after wave, peaking and cresting as he continued to lick and suck and caress at my center.

I came, my wetness flooding his hands, my inner muscles clenching as his fingers slid in and out. His tongue lapped at me, wringing out every last tremor until I collapsed back on the bed, spent.

"Oh, no. We're not nearly done yet," he whispered. Raising himself back above me he took my mouth and kissed me long and deep. I could taste myself on his tongue.

Nipping at my lower lip, I could feel him settle between my legs, his hardness probing my core. He slipped in and slid out, his tip teasing my ravenous opening. Then, finally, he did it. His thick cock slid inside, taunting me at first with barely half of himself, then retreating again until finally he buried as much of his shaft as could fit in me. I could feel the burn, my walls stretching to accommodate his girth, slick and welcoming as he claimed me deep within.

Almost immediately, I felt the wave rise again, taking me higher and higher. He started slow and then increased his speed. Sweat beaded on his forehead, and his back becoming slick under my hands. My fingers clawed for grip, matching him stroke for stroke as he pounded in and out, finding my spot every time without fail. We clung to each other until together we crested, his hardness exploding inside me as my walls trembled around him. I wrapped my arms around him as he shuddered out his release.

Chapter Twelve

KINSEY

*L*ying in Mason's arms afterwards, I felt safe, protected, and deeply loved. Stretching muscles I hadn't used in quite a while, I snuggled closer to his right side. He tightened his embrace around me, pillowing my head on his chest. My left hand played with the springy curls sprinkled across his well-defined muscles.

"What are you thinking about, Kinsey?" Bending his head, he looked me in the eye. "Are you okay?"

"I'm more than okay, I just... I was just wondering..." Pausing, I thought for a moment, then rolled out of his arms and lay looking at him. "I... is this real?" All the doubts I'd had came crowding back in. All the reasons we shouldn't be together flooded my mind, and the enormity of what we had done crashed over me.

He stiffened, "I don't know what this is, Kins." Then I felt him relax and his hand came up and he began stroking my hair. "I've never felt like this before." He whispered, voice cracking. "This time is different."

I pulled him close, pressing his head into my chest and

rubbing his back. He lay quietly, and I could feel his breath warm across my breast, my nipple alternating hot and cold in time with his breathing.

"I have never lost control like that before. You make me forget all the reasons we shouldn't be together."

"I know. It's that way for me too." My fingers danced in his hair, twirling the dark strands and standing them on end. "You make my previous relationships seem like child's play. My feelings for you scare me."

"They scare me too. I don't understand them." He leaned in for a long kiss before the intercom buzzed, interrupting the intimacy of the moment.

"Mr. Alexander, we are coming into some turbulence." The pilot's stern voice killed our magic. "If you could buckle yourselves in, that would be good."

MASON

The plane lurched and dropped, making my stomach rise until it felt like it was lodged in my throat. The turbulence threw me off the bed and onto the floor, wrenching me from the blissful spell I had been under. I landed in an ungainly heap, and reaching out to steady myself, tried to climb to my feet. This was not normal turbulence.

POW!

Whipping my head around and running to peer out the closest window, I could see black smoke trailing from the right engine. Orange flames licked the wing, singing the skin of the plane and leaving black bubbled metal behind.

Oh shit! This isn't good!

"Kinsey, get dressed fast. I need to check on the pilots." I threw the words over my shoulder, hoping she heard me as I raced to the front of the plane. The distance seemed much farther than I'd remembered.

"Guys, give me the short version." Slamming through the cockpit door, pulling on my pants as I went, the words tumbled out in a rush.

Ricardo, the pilot, didn't even look at me. Sweat beading on his brow, tension lines creasing his forehead, his knuckles white on the controls, he was the picture of concentration.

Matt, the first officer, paused briefly in his assessment of the disaster to fill me in. "It's bad, Mason. The right engine caught a bird or something. We're shutting it down."

Ricardo barely moved his lips and never took his eyes off the flickering instrument panel. "I don't know how bad the damage is yet," he said. "The instruments are going crazy, our stabilizers are gone, and we're fighting to keep altitude. Get strapped in. We may have to put her down the first chance we get."

"Okay. Keep me informed if you can. I'm going to warn Kinsey and get strapped in. Good luck." Closing my eyes, I said a silent prayer; the religion of my youth coming back to me even though I hadn't set foot in a church in more than a decade.

Ricardo and Matt had been with me for 5 years. Both former military pilots, they had retired after twenty years of service and moved into the private sector. I knew if anyone could pull off an emergency landing, it was them.

"Mason?" Kinsey came up behind me as I stood in the doorway, her eyes wide, projecting the terror she was fighting to keep inside. I turned to her, pulling the door shut at my back so she couldn't see the crew's panic.

"Kinsey, sit down and get buckled in. We've got problems." I gently turned her to the nearest seat. "We lost an engine." I didn't want to scare her, but I hadn't spotted any land yet—we were still somewhere over the gulf. "We have to be ready. We may be doing an emergency landing very soon." I hoped land was close, the Rolls Royce engines on this plane were work horses, but the plane was designed for two engines, and right now we only had one. Plus, I didn't know how damaged the wing was from the explosion and fire. If there was much structural damage, the plane might not hold up against the additional strain we were flying under.

She gasped, her eyes so big the whites were showing. All the color leached from her face, paling the rosy post-coital glow she'd had only moments before.

"What…" She swallowed rapidly. "What do we need to do?"

"We just need to be prepared. Get buckled. It's only going to get rougher." I snagged my shirt and shoes from the bedroom and finished getting dressed. It's like when you are little and your mom tells you to put on clean underwear just in case you are in an accident—I didn't want to crash half dressed. Kinsey and I both strapped ourselves into the leather club chairs where only an hour before we'd had such a relaxed meal.

Marie, our flight attendant, was with the pilots. I put on a headset so I could listen in on the conversation in the cockpit, while helping Kinsey secure her chest harness. Then, I pulled up our flight route on my iPad. I was relieved to see we were approaching the Central American coast. If we could just make it to land, there had to be an airport nearby. Central America isn't that wide. We might just make it.

Flipping over to the cockpit channel on the headset, the first thing I heard was, "God damn it! The left engine is starting to overheat! I'm going to lower the speed and set the best glide angle. Come on, baby, come on!" The stress was evident in Ricardo's voice as he continued, "She's getting harder to control. Matt, send out a mayday and find me the closest airport or… some place we can try to land."

I was glad Kinsey wasn't listening. The news up front wasn't good. I looked back at the iPad—we were closer to land, and it looked like we were just off the coast near the Honduras-Nicaragua border.

"MAYDAY! MAYDAY! This is Gulfstream 6301-November-Charlie! I repeat, this is Gulfstream 6301-November-Charlie—off the coast of Honduras! We have lost an engine and are making an emergency landing!" Matt's voice trembled as he ended the mayday transmission.

"The headwinds are getting worse. Do you want me to take the controls?" Matt asked Ricardo.

"No, I've got it. Keep working the radio. See if you can raise anyone," Ricardo said through clenched teeth. I could picture him, his face the picture of concentration as he muscled the plane into submission. "I'm descending. We should break through the clouds in a minute. Tell me the instant you see land and cross your fingers there's less head-wind below 18,000 feet."

The clouds were white against the window. They even looked peaceful, although, from the way the plane shuddered, I knew they were anything but. My hands gripped the armrests of the ivory leather chairs, and I saw Kinsey doing the same. Her face was drawn, her eyes huge and a dark, stormy blue, beseeching me to make this all right. I reached over and gently pried her fingers off the armrest one by one and squeezed her hand.

"We're going to be okay," I told her. "These guys are the best at what they do." Holding her hand, I prayed I could keep my promise and keep her safe.

"Mason, I'm scared." Her voice came out small, barely a whisper, the rattling and groaning of the plane almost drowning out her words.

"I know, baby. I know."

We suddenly broke through the clouds, the ocean spreading out below us. The deep blue of the gulf slowly gave way to the turquoise of shallower Central American waters. My eyes glued to the window, I thought I spotted something dark rising from the horizon.

"Kinsey, I think I see land!" Squeezing her hand in excitement, my heart lightened. For a moment, I enjoyed the feel of her smooth, unblemished skin against my calloused palms and the relief in her budding smile. Then reality crashed down, and I realized we weren't out of the woods yet.

"Where?" Her voice rose at the end, and her smile vanished as panic began to break through the iron control she held on her emotions.

"Look! Right there on the horizon!" With my free hand, I pointed at the dark speck, which grew larger as Ricardo and Matt brought us closer and closer to what I hoped would be safety.

KINSEY

"Oh my God, Mason! We're going to be okay!" My fingers tightened around his hand as I leaned toward the window, hungry for every glimpse of the shoreline as it came closer and closer. My whole body tensed with fear that we would crash into the dark gulf waters below and never be seen again. "I can see mountains and trees! Where are we? Is that the beach and jungle? Where are the houses? The airport —where is the airport?"

"Ricardo and Matt are looking for a safe place to land us —hopefully an airport, but really they're just looking for any place they might be able to put us down in one piece."

Searching the earth laid out below, I saw a thin white strip of beach and then trees. There was nothing but a thick green layer of trees. *There is no place to land!*

"Put us down? What are you saying? We might crash?!" I admit it—I panicked. I rarely read about plane crashes that ended with passengers walking away. Instead, I was used to newspapers and CNN with big photos showing pieces of the wreckage, accompanied by long lists of the dead.

"Mason?" Ricardo's voice interrupted us over the speaker

system. "I've got Matt looking for a clearing. This engine isn't going to make it to the airport in the capitol. I can't control the plane much longer. We're losing systems, and I'm afraid the wing is going to fracture."

"We hear you." Mason keyed the mike on his headset and turned to look at me. "Hold on, babe. It's going to be a bumpy landing."

"Aaaaaaaahhhh!" I lost it. I screamed. I yelled. I wailed in despair.

"Shhhh… shhhh… Kinsey, just hold on. Ricardo will get us on the ground safely. Just close your eyes. This will all be over soon."

That didn't make me feel any better. My imagination took over and I couldn't repress that primal urge to scream my head off as we plummeted lower and lower in the sky. My stomach rose, and the weightless feeling and a lack of control took over my nervous system and threw me into panic. Coming closer and closer to the water, we fell through space until suddenly treetops whipped by the window, accompanied by the wrenching sounds of tearing metal. Mason and I were thrown around, our seat belts and harnesses holding us back against our seats as everything not tied down flew up and hit the ceiling. The glasses broke. Food flew all around us. Files and documents scattered like oversized confetti.

The plane shuddered beneath our feet, and my teeth rattled as we hit the trees. I heard a window breaking some-where, and I was violently thrown around in my seat. Smoke filled the cabin, obscuring my view and choking me. Blackness shuttered my eyes, and I remember nothing else.

Chapter Thirteen

KINSEY

$\mathcal{T}$he sounds of chirping birds waking me quickly took a backseat to the massive headache throbbing behind my eyes. *Oh man!* I cradled my head in my hands, praying the pain would stop.

I opened my eyes, and my surroundings slowly came into focus. *Where am I?* Looking down, I found myself strapped into an off-white leather chair, looking out through a gaping, shredded hole at nothing but jungle.

Pulling on the seat belt, I released myself from the safety restraints and tried to stand. Wobbling under me, my legs were so weak I had to sit back down. Then the memories came flooding back. Mason and I had been flying to China for an important meeting. We had a passionate encounter, and then the plane... the plane... something happened... We crashed.

OH MY GOD! WE CRASHED!

Panicking, I looked around for Mason.

Where is he? I tried standing again, and this time my legs held me. Putting my hand to my aching head, I was startled when it came back bloody. I must have taken quite a hit when we crashed.

I picked up a spoon that had landed on the floor and looked at my distorted reflection. I had a big gash across my left cheek and a good sized knot on my temple. Grabbing a napkin by my feet, I held it to my face and tried to stop the flow of blood.

When I looked beyond my reflection, I gasped at the broken shell of the plane. I was in the middle section of the fuselage. All the windows were broken. The cutlery and table-ware were strewn everywhere. The presentation Mason and I had stayed up all night carefully piecing together lay scattered all around me.

The seat Mason had been in was gone; only a hole in the floor remained where it had been ripped out. Looking outside, I spotted the nose of the plane at the end of a deep groove gouged out of the dirt. Bits and shards of the magnificent jet now littered the jungle around us.

I jumped awkwardly off the torn, exposed edge of the plane, and my skirt tore with a loud *RIP!* Landing crookedly in my heels on the soft, loamy earth, I began to sweat. My drooping hair stuck in damp strings to my face and neck.

The smell of decomposing jungle matter filled my nostrils. *We must be deep in the jungle somewhere.* I didn't even know what country we had aimed for when we started our emergency descent.

My heels, unsuited for jungle walking, kept getting stuck in the dirt, but I labored on. I *had* to find Mason. Staggering as best I could, I hobbled the 50 yards to the front of the plane, and climbed up to reach the doorknob. It was locked.

BANG! BANG! BANG!

I hammered on the cockpit door and looked around for something to break in with. It seemed silly that the door was intact when the cockpit wasn't even attached to the plane.

I spotted a fire extinguisher lying in the dirt. It must have fallen out of the plane when it broke apart. I grabbed it and started pounding it against the door. "Hello! Hello! Can you hear me?! Hello?! Is anyone in there?"

Wham! Wham! Wham!

The door began to splinter and finally broke apart. It gave way so suddenly I fell into the cockpit, catching myself on the back of the pilot's seat.

Gah!

I gagged, staggered to the door, and puked. They were both dead. At least, I thought they had to be dead. Ricardo had been impaled by a tree branch through his chest, and Matt had been hit with something so big half his face was caved in. I had never seen a dead body before, and I never wanted to again. They were limp and pale, all the vibrance drained from them and lying in a puddle of dark red blood that pooled under their seats. Marie, the stewardess, had been thrown through the front window. Through the shards of broken glass, I could see her hanging lifeless upside down from a tree.

There was nothing I could do here. They were all beyond help, but Mason—I still had hope for Mason. I hadn't found him yet. He could have been okay. I couldn't be the only person alive in this jungle. That was unthinkable.

Jumping out of the cockpit and back onto the soft loamy dirt, my heel got caught in a root and I fell, skinning my knees.

Oof!

"Shit!" I rolled over and sat up. Brushing the dirt and debris from my hands and knees, I gathered my wits and pulled off the expensive shoes Mason had bought me. I took one last look at the gorgeous five-inch patent leather Christian Louboutin stiletto peep-toe pumps with the sexy red soles, and sparing three seconds to mourn their loss, I snapped the heels off both shoes. Slipping them back on, I walked easier, and my feet were still protected as I searched for Mason.

I started looking around the main section of the fuselage

where I had woken after the crash. I checked the piles of wreckage, slowly making larger and larger circles away from my seat so I wouldn't miss any sign of Mason. Stumbling around, I tried not to cut myself on the jagged edges of smoking metal or trip on any of the lumpy roots that stuck up from the soil and twisted through the dirt.

I stepped carefully along the deep scar left by the plane sliding through the jungle, which had created the only open space in the thick vegetation. The further I got from the plane, the harder it was to search. The plants closed in and covered every square inch of land. At least the jungle canopy created a cooling shade cover, providing some relief from the unforgiving equatorial sun and oppressive humidity.

Water dripped from green leaves the size of umbrellas. A rat's nest of vines dangled from and connected towering trees. Some were so large it would take three or four people holding hands to wrap their arms around the entire trunk.

Something caught my eye, and I fought my way through the vines to a rotting log. Something big was on the other side of it, something with straight edges. I was discovering straight edges were an oddity in the jungle.

"Mason!" I cried. Finally making it to the other side of the rotting log, I found him in a steaming pool of sunshine, still strapped into his seat, laying on his back, eyes closed. With a quick glance, I took in the length of him. He appeared unharmed but for a few scrapes here and there. No major injuries were visible.

Falling to my sore knees next to him, I felt for a pulse. *He's alive!* I ran my hands along his arms and legs, feeling for lumps or breaks. I didn't find any malformations, but he had a nasty knot on his head. Rocking back on my heels, I closed my eyes and sighed in relief. A single tear trickled down my dirty cheek.

"Mason!" I shook him frantically to wake him up, but nothing happened. Sobbing in relief that I had found him alive, I tried to drag him under a tree and out of the sun. He was too heavy and awkward, and the chair, still bolted to the cabin floor, kept me from moving him. I unhooked his belt and harness, and he fell from the chair, face down. Heaving him over on to his back, I again tried to drag him over to a tree. This time, he slowly slid across the wet leaves as I staggered backwards, holding tight to his wrists and trying not to knock his head against any stumps or rocks sticking up from the jungle floor. I propped him up against the tree, out of the sun.

Sitting next to him, holding his hand, I let my eyes roam across his face. Even unconscious he made my heart skip a beat with his strong jaw, the stubble across it darker than I had ever seen it. His eyes were closed now, but when awake he'd looked at me with such emotion, allowing me a brief window into his psyche. Shoulders were broad enough to carry the world now relaxed.

What should I do? We were maybe 500 feet from the main section of the airplane fuselage, which was still mostly intact. If I was going to be stuck in the jungle with an unconscious Mason, I wanted the protection offered by the body of the plane. But, Mason was twice my size and currently an unhelpful, unconscious lump of dead weight. Even dragging him five feet to the tree had exhausted me. I wouldn't be able to drag him the same way back to the plane.

"You better wake up soon," I told him as though he could hear. "And you better be in a condition to help me. We have to figure out how to get out of here. I haven't seen what lives here yet, but I do watch the Discovery Channel, and I know there are animals with big sharp teeth that will come out tonight."

Clenching my jaw, I stood. "You stay right here, I'll be back in a minute. I've got to find something to help me move you." I gingerly walked back to the plane, picking my way back through the wreckage of the crash, and started looking for something, *anything* I could use to move him. I needed something Mason-sized, but light enough for me to pull. And I needed better clothes. Even torn up the thigh, my skirt was restrictive, and my blouse was already in tatters. And though snapping the heels off my Louboutin's had made walking somewhat easier, my poor shoes weren't designed for this terrain.

I climbed up inside the plane and carefully made my way back to the bedroom. Our suitcases had been thrown about but were still intact, so I dug out some skinny jeans, tennis shoes, and a t-shirt I had brought to sleep in. The outfit wasn't fashionable, but it was a whole lot more practical. I changed quickly and pulled my hair back in a ponytail.

Leaving the room, I looked around. I mean *really* looked around. I let my eyes travel across everything with a purpose.

My phone!

Spotting my cell phone sticking out from beneath some rubble in the corner of the cabin, I ran over and grabbed it. I cradled it like a precious gift, kissed it, swiped it open, and tried to call the office. I couldn't believe I hadn't thought to call for help sooner.

Calling office, the screen said.

Nothing happened; I had no signal. I hadn't thought there would be cell towers in the middle of the jungle, but I'd hoped we were close enough to a town to pick something up. *God damn it!* Hope is a fickle thing, and seeing my phone had given me hope.

I slipped it into my pocket, enjoying its comforting weight. I picked up and considered a tablecloth before dropping it again. Pulling Mason over flat ground, a tablecloth might have worked, but it was less useful in the rolling dirt and boulder strewn mountains we had crashed into. I pulled all kinds of things out of cupboards: parachutes, a first aid kit, an emergency raft for water landings. There were lots of useful things *if* Mason ever woke up. They were no use to me while he was unconscious.

Standing up and putting my hands on my hips, I let out a frustrated sigh. Then my eyes fell on the outside wall of the cockpit that sat abandoned across the clearing. There was a backboard strapped to the wall.

"**A**lright Mason, I'm back," I announced cheerfully, as I made it back to the tree he was lying under. I had a backpack thrown over my shoulder and was dragging the backboard behind me.

"Now, don't fight me on this. I know someone as big and strong as you won't want to lie quietly on this board while I haul you back to the plane, but humor me." For my sanity I had to pretend he could hear me. I didn't have the luxury of time for a nervous breakdown, and pretending this was all normal was my only other option. The sun was sinking below the tree line and darkness was fast approaching. We both needed to be somewhere safe and protected before the nocturnal creatures in the jungle came out to feed. I was already seeing more and more mosquitos, those dastardly little blood suckers. There was no time to waste.

"Help me, Mason. Roll over onto this board," I said as I muscled his unconscious form to lie on the board. After a short and exhausting struggle, I secured the straps around him to hold him in place.

I needed a moment to catch my breath before taking a length of rope I'd found in a cabinet, and making a V-shaped bridle, which I attached to the head of the board on the left and right sides. I then attached that to a backpack I wore backward, creating a harness that allowed me to pull the board with my whole body. Then, I gingerly started back to the plane, trying to pick the smoothest dirt and flattest terrain to haul my load across.

It was slow going, but tolerable that way. It took over an hour to go the winding 500 feet through the jungle, but we finally arrived back at the plane. I climbed up onto the ledge made by the cabin floor, about four feet off the ground, and took off the backpack, tying the rope attached to it to a handle inside the plane. Then, leaning the head of the board on the ledge and resting the foot of it on the ground, I kept it from falling by tying it in place with the rope. Hopping back to the ground, sweaty and covered in dirt, my muscles shook like I had just climbed the toughest route at the gym, I bent down and heaved the foot of the board up into the plane, using the edge of the exposed floor to pivot the head of it so I could slide the board flat into the cabin. *If only my dad could see me now. I don't think he would even recognize me.* Sweaty, stringy hair, filthy and unfashionable clothes, no makeup, a bloody and swollen cheek, and covered in mosquito bites, I barely recognized myself.

I dragged Mason back to the bedroom, unstrapped him from the board, laid him out on the floor, and covered him up to his chin with a sheet from the bed. Closing the bedroom door, I surveyed the wreckage of the fuselage. I needed to close us in to keep the animals and bugs out, but didn't have a lot to work with. The bedroom door would help, but I wanted something more.

Spying a parachute I had discarded earlier, I knelt down and started pulling the chute out of its pack. "I think this will work, Mason. The chute is big enough to cover the open end of the fuselage, and I can secure it in place with duct tape. That'll at least keep the mosquitos out." I was rather pleased with my own ingenuity.

"What? You don't think it's enough? Well, either you get up and help me, or we do it my way." I looked back at the bedroom like I was expecting an answer. I kept hoping he would wake up.

"No? You're not gonna help? Okay, then quit complaining." I set about taping the parachute along the top edge of the fuselage so it hung down and covered the opening. I finally secured the last edge in place using up almost the entire roll of tape, but I was satisfied it was not going anywhere. It would keep out rain and bugs and hopefully deter anything larger from sneaking in.

Sitting down in the only chair left in the living area, the one I had been sitting in when we crashed, I listened to the night sounds of the jungle as the sun slipped below the horizon. I separated out the sounds of monkeys chattering as they traveled from tree to tree above our heads. I heard several different birds. Some so close they could be right outside the plane, and others sounding like they came from far away treetops.

As I sat there resting, things started to hurt. I felt bruising on my waist and chest from the seat belt and harness. My hands, knees, and feet transmitted pain from every cut and scrape I had gotten since we crashed.

"Kinsey?" I almost didn't react as the weak voice interrupted my reverie. I had been imagining talking to Mason, so hearing his voice calling from the bedroom, I just assumed it was my mind playing tricks on me.

"Kinsey? You there?" The call came again, stronger, and I realized it wasn't my imagination.

"Mason?! You're awake!" Running to the bedroom, I slammed open the door. There he was, awake and sitting up. I collapsed into his waiting arms.

Chapter Fourteen

MASON

*W*hen I woke up lying on a backboard on the floor of the Gulfstream, I was a little confused.

Calling out for Kinsey, I heard her respond from the cabin, and then she came flying through the door and collapsed into my arms in a puddle of tears. Five minutes passed, and she still hadn't stopped crying. Her whole body shook with big, heart-wrenching sobs. A couple of times she tried to speak, but couldn't seem to form words.

"Shhh, Kinsey. Shhh. It's going to be okay. We're alive. We're both alive."

"Bah-da-pla-cr-and..." Her words were garbled, incomprehensible. Her nose ran like a faucet. With her eyes pinched shut, tears streamed down her face and soaked my wrinkled shirt. I rubbed her back, making slow, soothing circles as she hiccupped and sobbed. Eventually, her breathing slowed and she managed to get herself under control.

Just like when I'd bumped into her coming out of the elevator at her dad's office, she looked up at me, her big blue eyes swimming with tears. "Thank you for waking up, for not leaving me here alone."

I started to stand up so I could move her to the more comfortable bed and look outside, but she pulled me back down and climbed into my lap. "No! Wait, Mason! Don't go out yet."

"Where are we, Kinsey?" I really needed to know where we were and what condition everyone was in. I needed to find Ricardo, Matt, and Marie and ask them what they remembered.

"We crashed somewhere in the jungle." She sniffed and wiped her nose on her sleeve. "They're dead. They're all dead. The pilots. Marie. It's just us."

"Help me up. I want to see." I set her off my lap and slowly started to get up again. Grabbing onto the bed for support as one ankle threatened to buckle, I made my way to the door.

"Mason, wait." Kinsey followed me as I looked through the door at the rest of the plane, which wasn't there. The floor and ceiling ended about fifteen feet from the bedroom door, just past the one remaining chair. The jagged edge of the fuselage was covered in a thin opaque material, loose and rippling in the wind. The hole in the floor where my chair had been was covered in a garbage bag. Silverware, books, clothes, leaves, dirt, and bits of airplane were strewn across what had once been a beautiful Persian rug. The remaining windows were cracked, and I couldn't see much more than blackness outside. The jungle was *that* dark. We had to be really far from civilization for there to be absolutely no ambient light visible.

"What's out there?" I asked her, unable see anything out the window.

"Jungle. I never saw anything but jungle."

Bracing myself against the wall, I sank down to the floor and pulled her down with me. Tucking her against my side and pulling her close, I buried my nose in her hair. She was sweaty and dirty, but her hair still held the faint scent of her strawberry shampoo. I felt myself stirring and tamped down that response. *This isn't the time.* We could explore our feelings for one another later if we ever got out of there alive. "Kinsey, I want you to go into the next room and go to sleep."

"No, Mason," she started to protest.

"Kinsey, you are exhausted, and I just woke up. You've done a great job taking care of me and keeping us safe. Now let me take care of you. I want to look around here in the plane. I won't leave it, but I want to take stock of what we have. I'll come to bed in a little bit."

I t took a while, but I finally convinced Kinsey to lie down. She was emotionally and physically exhausted after the day's events. I ended up sitting on the bed next to her, rubbing her back until she finally drifted off. I had never been in this position with a woman before, never wanted to take care of them. The feeling was new and unsettling, but then again, so was Kinsey. In just a few weeks, she had completely turned my staid, boring life upside down.

I still don't really understand how she managed to haul my 200 pounds of dead weight from where she'd found me and got me up into the plane, but I was definitely impressed by her ingenuity and tenacity. She had really stepped up to the plate better than I ever imagined a sheltered, pampered twenty-one-year-old could. I was twice her size, and after a plane crash and discovering everyone else was dead, I'm not sure I would have done as well.

Limping around the small space, I took stock of our situation. Once morning came and there was enough light to see, I would check outside, but for now, I would have to be happy with the contents of the fuselage.

The coolers along the walls had some bottled water,

granola bars, and bags of mixed nuts, along with mini alcohol bottles. The remains of our meal lay strewn across the floor. We had one remaining parachute, the backpack Kinsey had used when hauling me, a flashlight, a fire extinguisher, and our luggage in the bedroom. It wasn't a lot to work with, but I was confident we could figure something out.

My knees creaked as I stood to retrieve the first aid kit. I wasn't going to be much good tomorrow if I didn't treat my sprained ankle and get some rest too. After just an hour or so awake, I was already exhausted, likely a side effect from the concussion and time spent unconscious.

I wrapped my ankle tightly, which made it was much easier to walk on. Reaching into a pocket on the wall next to where I had been sitting during the flight, I pulled out my iPad. I said a silent prayer of thanks that it was there and functional.

Then I settled into the only chair left and pulled up the route tracking software. The GPS in the iPad still connected to satellites for location data even when there was no cellular service, and based on the flight map, we were nowhere near cellular service. The dot put us on the Honduras-Nicaragua border, smack in the middle of the Bosawás Biosphere Reserve, a largely unexplored area. It was one of the worst places to crash. We were miles from anything remotely resembling civilization. I had no idea how we were going to get out of there. Hopefully, I could figure something out in the morning.

I quietly hobbled into the bedroom, shut the door behind me, and eased into bed next to a sleeping Kinsey. She was cute, looking much more relaxed in sleep than she had when I woke up earlier. The remains of dried tears glistened on her cheeks, but the worried groove between her eyebrows had relaxed, and she looked closer to sixteen than her twenty-one years.

Pulling her close, I wrapped my arms around her and

rested her head on my bicep. I spooned her from behind, nestling my hard-on into the cleft of her cheeks, and fell into a deep and dreamless sleep.

~

The jungle rose early. The sounds of parrots squawking as they flew from tree to tree woke me up shortly after sunrise. The piercing cry of howler monkeys echoed through the vegetation, and I heard the roar of a jungle cat coming from somewhere not far off.

Easing my arm out from under Kinsey, I rolled to the edge of the bed and sat up. Dizzy for a moment, I gently probed the knot on my head. It seemed a little less swollen, and my headache was mostly gone. *What I wouldn't give for a hot shower right about now!*

I stood up a little unsteadily, but my ankle held while I tiptoed out of the bedroom. Loosening the tape on one side of the parachute, I carefully hopped down out of the plane and took my first look at the crash scene.

I had to grab on to the side of the fuselage to keep from falling. There were pieces of jagged metal, broken trees, and charred remains of engine everywhere. Some were big pieces like the tail we'd slept in while others were no bigger than my fist. *Oh my god… It's a miracle we survived.*

I carefully picked my way through the wreckage to the cockpit. Not even 24 hours had passed since the crash, but Ricardo and Matt were already starting to smell. Eyes watering, I climbed up through the cockpit door and quickly searched for anything useful. I wrestled the crash ax off the wall behind the left seat. Breathing through my mouth, I went through the pilots' pockets and the cockpit around them. The co-pilot had a tiny Swiss army knife in his pants pocket, and around him, I found another flashlight, a couple bottles of water, a bottle of ibuprofen, and a pair of sunglasses. I took

Marie's purse for Kinsey. Marie wouldn't be using it anymore. After tossing the stuff I found inside, I threw Marie's catchall over my shoulder and carefully made my way back to Kinsey, dropping it by the one remaining club chair before silently slipping back into the bedroom.

Leaning on one elbow, I reached over and brushed Kinsey's hair out of her face. She was so beautiful, and she was sleeping so soundly I really hated to wake her up.

"Kinsey." I gently shook her shoulder. "Kinsey, wake up."

"Grmmmunmph," She rolled away from me, burying her face in a pillow.

"Babe, we need to get going." I shook her a little more forcefully this time, and her eyelids fluttered.

"Mmmph. What time is it? I just want to sleep a little longer." Burrowing deeper in the soft mattress, she made it obvious she wasn't a morning person.

"Kinsey! I need your help! Remember the plane crash?"

She suddenly sat up, and I dodged just in time to avoid her head connecting with my nose. "Oh my god! I can't believe I fell asleep!" Wide awake now, she looked at me, a question in her eyes.

KINSEY

Mason jerked me from a sound sleep. I was dreaming we were at a resort in the Caribbean with palm trees, sunscreen, and coconuts. Waking up to reality was rough; I preferred the dream.

In the harsh reality of daylight, I threw myself at Mason, and he enveloped me in a hug. I took a minute to get myself together, enjoying the feel of his strong arms around me. He made me feel safe and protected. It was a fleeting feeling, but denial is a strong motivator.

Leaning back, I left the warm circle of his arms and

suddenly felt cold despite the jungle's heat already penetrating the metal shell of the plane's remains. "What are we going to do?" I asked Mason. "How long do you think it will be before they will find us?"

"I don't know, Kinsey," he said. "They might not."

"What do you mean, 'they might not?' They might not find us?" That thought had never occurred to me. They *had* to find us. Weren't there people in control towers all across the world watching airplanes on radar?

"Well, we are in the middle of the jungle. Somewhere on the border of Honduras and Nicaragua, much of which is largely unexplored. Neither country has the resources to come find us. Back home they will have a general idea where we are, but they won't know our exact location. It's a large area to search, and often crashes like this are never found. The jungle will quickly recover and grow up over the plane, and 50 years from now, some hikers will stumble across it. I don't want to still be here when that happens. We have limited food and water, so we can't just sit here and wait."

I had nothing to say to that. Wordlessly rolling out of bed, I groaned as the muscles I had over-used the previous day began to ache. Slipping on my underwear, I turned to face Mason. We had to get out of there. "Ok, what do we need to do?"

"We need to make a plan. We need food, water, and shelter, and it all needs to be portable. This tail section is great, it's comfortable and protected, but we can't take it with us." He started pacing, his limp barely noticeable as he counted things off on his fingers.

I dug a notebook out of my carry-on and started taking notes.

"What are you doing?" he asked.

"Writing this down. I don't want to forget anything."

He laughed. "Ever the organized one. Ok, let's see what we have." He leaned down and grabbed our luggage, which had fallen in a pile on the floor. He tossed the bags and suit-cases on the bed. Unzipping them, he started digging around and throwing things in piles. "Ties, suit coats, dress shoes, worthless… ah! My gym shoes, I'll wear these."

Setting down my notebook, I pulled my suitcase close, unzipped it, and started sorting. "Well, my Manolo Blahniks won't do me any good, but I do have a windbreaker." Digging through, I discarded almost everything—my skirts and blouses, my makeup. *Wait!* I grabbed a pink toiletry bag from the pile and unzipped it. "I have a bottle of sunscreen and hand sanitizer!"

"Good finds, Kinsey." He smiled at me and we added them to his keep pile. We ended up with comfortable jeans, t-shirts, and athletic shoes for both of us. I kept a long sleeve blouse and windbreaker. Mason had a baseball cap, a hand towel, and a long-sleeve running shirt.

We dumped the whole first aid kit into the backpack and added my sunscreen, hand sanitizer, and some soap. Moving into the other room, we started digging through the food.

Mason put together a bag full of water bottles and non-perishable foods. "None of this cheese or fruit will keep," he told me. "We should probably eat it, and save the wrapped stuff for traveling."

I nodded. "Okay. Let me see what else I can put together. There's some orange juice here, and some muffins too."

Spreading a tablecloth out on the floor, I laid out our feast, and we took a break to stuff ourselves silly with everything we couldn't take with us.

Chapter Fifteen

MASON

*D*igging graves is hot, sweaty work. I never thought I would be a gravedigger, but there I was, covered in dirt and digging a hole in the jungle floor the day after waking up from a plane crash.

"We can't just leave them here Mason; not like this." That's what Kinsey had said to me two hours earlier, and that's how I ended up shirtless, sweat streaming down my back, sunburned and digging graves in the jungle. I was rethinking agreeing with Kinsey. *Is it too late to change my mind?*

I sure hoped Ricardo and Matt were looking down on us and appreciating the work we put into burying them. Unfortunately, I had a feeling Ricardo was pointing and laughing at me, wondering why in the hell I was digging a friggin' hole in the middle of the jungle instead of hiking my ass out of there. He was way too practical for that. He'd have said, "Mason, I'm dead. Who the hell cares where my body decomposes? I'm in an airplane, which was my favorite place to be. Planting my ass in the ground for flowers to grow on is for you, not me."

"I think that about does it." I leaned on the makeshift shovel I'd made from a chunk of palm frond and the emergency axe. My hands were red and raw, but I had three person-sized holes in the ground for my three dead friends.

"Ugh," Kinsey said. She flicked her wrists and tried to shake off the squishy bits sticking to her hands as we dragged the last body into its grave. "Some of his skin came off on me."

"We got them into the ground just in time. Any later and we would be moving them in pieces." Stinky, gassy, gross pieces we'd toss in the ground for the jungle to eat. With the proliferation of bugs and other decomposers, the high heat, and oppressive humidity, the bodies would be recycled back to earth very quickly.

"I just met them, but I didn't want to remember them like this." Kinsey sniffed, wiping away a tear. "But I'm glad we did this. I hate to think what would happen to them if we left them out in the open."

Scooping the last of the dirt on top of the three piles, Kinsey ceremoniously placed three small crosses and flowers on the top of each mound. She had used Ricardo's eyeglasses to burn their names into the bits of wood she had fashioned into crosses of sorts.

I tossed the hated palm-frond shovel off into the bushes. I never wanted to dig anything again.

"I think it's too late to leave today," I said. "We should start out at first light." I was still cleaning up after the hot, sweaty work of burying my friends. "I need to patch up my hands. I don't want the blisters to get infected, and in this mess, they could."

"Let me take a look," she demanded. I held them out, and she took them, flipped them over, and winced. "You are a mess. I guess that palm frond wasn't the best shovel." Pouring a little of our precious water over them, she carefully dabbed at my wounds with a clean towel, wiping away the dirt bit by bit, exposing the blisters.

Her big blue eyes looked up at me through the thick fringe of eyelashes as she worked. I shivered; even in my exhausted state, I wanted her. I felt a connection to her—a connection I seemed to have with her and no one else.

"Have you figured out where we are yet?" Her innocent question woke me from my dreamy desire. "Are we close to a town, you think?"

"I'm having a hard time figuring anything more specific than 'somewhere on the Nicaragua-Honduras border.'" Gently pulling my newly wrapped hands from her grasp, I picked up the compass I had removed from the cockpit dash and held it up. "We watched the sun rise over there this morning, and the compass agrees that is east." I pointed through the jungle.

I laid out a close-up section of an aviation map and spread it out on the dirty carpet. "This shows where all the airports are in this part of Central America. See those magenta circles and those magenta runways?"

"These?" she asked, touching several spots on the map.

"Yes." I paused and let her look a little more. "Now, see this big empty space over here?"

"Yeeeeesss...?" This was a slower, more drawn out agreement, and I could see the question in her eyes.

"That's where I think we are."

Raising her eyebrow even further, she said nothing. She just looked at me to continue. Instead, I pulled out Ricardo's cell phone and held it up.

"We have no service Mason, what is that going to do?"

"Well, look at this." I pulled up one of the aviation apps Ricardo used and showed her the basic map on her phone. "Both apps show us smack in the middle of the reserve in the northern part of Jinotega, here on the north border of Nicaragua."

"I don't know much about that area," Kinsey said, laser focused on the maps in her hands.

"Neither do I, but it's my understanding this is a largely unexplored area." I was trying to downplay my concerns, but it looked like I shouldn't have been worried. The scientist in Kinsey was emerging.

"Looking at the map, it's pretty hilly, probably a rain forest —most of this area is." She settled cross-legged on the floor and zoomed in on the area. "And that's a significant chunk of Nicaragua. What is that—ten percent? Twenty percent of the country?"

"It's a big part. We are slightly to the east, and that seems to be the best direction to go."

"Yeah," she said and added almost as an afterthought, "and if we head downhill we have to hit water some time." She looked at the phones again. "Neither one is fully charged. They aren't going to last long."

"I know, but at least they confirmed my suspicions. It looks like if we go far enough east, we will eventually hit a river we can follow to the sea."

She thought about it, and replied, "Yeah, we should do that. It will be easier to follow than the compass."

Kinsey never ceased to surprise me. She seemed to instinctively know my thoughts.

Finishing with her study of the two maps, she shut both phones down. "Let's get one more good night of rest. We should probably leave first thing in the morning." She tossed me the phones to tuck in my pack. "And we should both check each other out for injuries."

"You just want me naked again!" I said, wiggling my eyebrows lasciviously.

Laughing, she playfully smacked my arm. "You are terrible. I know I hurt, but it's hard to tell if anything is serious.

We might want to do that daily, so like you said, nothing gets out of hand." She pointed at the backpacks. "And I want to repack our bags to make sure the weight is distributed properly."

"I'll take care of the bags." I wanted to shift some of the heavier items into mine. She didn't need to carry that much weight.

"Have you ever backpacked before?" Kinsey asked me, raising one eyebrow in question.

"Not really. I mean, I've carried a backpack before... back when I was in school."

"That's not the same," Kinsey replied. "I'm talking about carrying 30 to 50 pounds on your back for ten hours a day, day after day. Have you ever done THAT?"

"No." I hated admitting I wasn't good at something.

"Then it's settled. I will pack the bags so they carry the best. We are taking a lot of heavy stuff and those aren't hiking packs. They are going to be uncomfortable, but I don't want to leave anything behind."

"Why don't you just let me carry it all? I'm bigger." *And stronger,* I thought, although I didn't say that.

"No, Mason. I will carry half. Neither of us is in top fighting form. We really have no idea where we are, how far we are from where we are going, and God forbid if something happens to you, if we get separated, if *anything,* I want to be able to take care of myself. I won't be dependent upon you." She stood there, eyes blazing, hair in a wild golden halo around her head. She reminded me of an Amazon—a short Amazon, but an Amazon. Fierce, strong, determined.

Chapter Sixteen

KINSEY

$\mathcal{M}$ason was infuriating me. Just like my father, he was treating me as if I was a child who didn't know anything.

Of course I didn't know *everything*, but I could read a map and the writing on the wall. The maps from the plane were designed to be used from the air. They would be little help on the ground. The phones would die within 24 hours, maybe 48 if we used them sparingly. They had less than half a charge as it was, and we had no way to power them. Forget phone apps, there would be no following the blinking blue ball in this jungle.

In the past, I may have been content to rely on others, to let them take care of me. I may have played at college, at getting my degree, telling myself I was going to show my father what I was capable of and make a splash in the biotech world, but I didn't even know what I was capable of back then. Having only recently been cut off and forced to grow up, I was just beginning to discover myself.

This situation in the jungle—I could do this. I wasn't

going to die in the middle of nowhere, dirty, tired, and sore. No. I was going to get out of there. With Mason's help, we were going to survive. I wasn't going to be dependent on him, though. My background in science and my time rock climbing, hiking, and backpacking had provided invaluable knowledge for the situation we were in. He was smart, but racquetball and gym workouts were no match for Mother Nature. He may not have realized it yet, but he needed me just as much as I needed him.

Snuggling down with Mason, I burrowed into his side. His arm wrapped around my shoulders, and my hand smoothed over the light dusting of dark hair on his chest. Twirling my fingers around his belly button, I roamed his body as my mind wandered. I thought about everything we had already been through and wondered what was to come.

"If you keep doing that, Kinsey, we aren't going to get much sleep." Mason chuckled, and his voice rumbled in my ear.

"Mmmmm." I wriggled in his arms, my fingers dancing lower and lower, dipping below the sheet to bury themselves in the thicker curls surrounding his manhood. "Do we really need to sleep?"

"Maybe not," he said, his hand caressing up and down my shoulder and arm. I continued my explorations, and his hips began to move in time with my ministrations. The next hour we didn't do much talking.

~

Waking up our second morning in the jungle, the day started much like the first. The jungle was just as wild, just as noisy, just as hot, and just as humid as the day before.

Lying with my arm draped over Mason's waist and my head resting on his shoulder, I tried pretend we were waking up on a lazy Sunday morning in my apartment, but I couldn't. The fantasy just wasn't enough to make me forget our brutal reality.

Everything hurt, and I felt sticky and dirty. Dragging myself out of bed, I pulled on my dirty, sweaty clothes from the day before. I hadn't packed a whole lot of jungle trekking attire, so I just had what I was wearing. The saving grace was a pair of clean underwear I was saving.

I think the aches and pains from the crash hurt more that morning than they had the day before. I didn't have any adrenaline running through my veins this morning to help me forget. Moving like I was 61 instead of 21, I gingerly walked to the jagged edge of the plane, pulled back the parachute curtain, and sat down to look out with my legs dangling over the edge.

The jungle really was beautiful in a wild, untamed way. Parakeets flitted from tree to tree, their bright green bodies blending in with the lush green foliage. I heard a troop of howler monkeys go by. It was probably the same family that went by us yesterday about the same time. I heard the crunching and clicking of millions of bugs and beetles, feasting on jungle decay.

Scooting back just a bit so I was on the carpet, I sat cross-legged, my hands resting on my knees, and closed by eyes to center myself. I sensed the day growing brighter through my closed eyelids, and I could feel the sun rising through the trees as I silently performed my morning yoga routine.

What started as a way to deal with stress, recommended by one of the many shrinks my dad had sent me to over the years, had become a way of life. I started every day stretching my muscles, lengthening and strengthening, while silently meditating. I found it energized me. I started the day more alert, calmer, and a much happier person overall. It helped save my sanity when Dad cut me off a month ago, and hopefully it would keep me grounded now.

I sensed Mason's presence when he came out of the bedroom. Quietly, he came up next to me and began to imitate my sun salutations. Not a word was exchanged as we moved together in perfect harmony in the middle of the jungle. Stretching, posing on the ratty airplane carpet a million miles from home, the familiar movements calmed me, giving me a brief taste of normalcy in my now-chaotic, unpredictable world.

Slowly finishing my routine, I came back and settled into my cross-legged starting position. Mason and I sat like that for a few minutes before breaking the silence.

MASON

M oving with Kinsey, imitating her poses, I had never felt so in tune with a woman before. Yoga wasn't my thing. I enjoyed more competitive sports like racquetball, lacrosse, and rugby, but doing yoga with Kinsey in the early morning light felt spiritual. It was an intimacy I had never shared before. Closer than sex, it felt like a form of love making. Our bodies were perfectly synchronized.

If only my mother were here to see me now.

That's when I, Mason Alexander, confirmed bachelor, realized I was in love with spunky, quirky, klutzy Kinsey Hendrix, daughter of my mentor. If we made it out of the jungle alive, Noah was going to kill me.

Shivering, I remembered the slow, painful death Noah had always described for any man who dared touch his daughter.

S he handed me a bottle of water and a two-day-old roll stuffed with a limp piece of cheese and a pre-cooked sausage patty. Then, Kinsey shouldered her pack and looked at me expectantly.

"Yes, yes. I'm ready." Who would have expected pampered princess Kinsey Hendrix to be an avid backpacker? I know she told me that was something she did on weekends, but I had no idea she spent summers on the Appalachian Trail and had once hiked almost 1800 miles of it. Giving her a chaste kiss on the cheek, I tucked the sandwich into a pocket and helped her hop down out of the plane.

I held up the dash-mounted compass I had removed from the cockpit and oriented myself to east. "We walk that way." I pointed through the trees.

Kinsey focused on the compass in my hand and nodded. "East." Aimed in that direction, she took the compass from me, hitched her pack a little higher and hiked out of the clearing and into the wilds of the jungle. "How about I lead for a while?" She called back over her shoulder. Her footsteps were sure and unwavering, setting a pace I was going to have trouble keeping up with. This was clearly not her first time walking in the woods.

KINSEY

N ervously leading us east, I walked ahead so Mason wouldn't see my unease. The sun was high and brutal, and the air was almost thick enough to chew. We were flanked by a chorus of howler monkeys. I was used to the wilds of New York City, but this was new and frightening. I noticed a long line of leaf-cutter ants running in a line, each carrying a piece of leaf larger than itself. Marching in the direction we were traveling, they were fascinating to watch.

Within an hour of leaving the shelter of the plane, we encountered our first mud hole. "Careful, Kinsey." Mason moved to go ahead of me.

"No, Mason. Let me," I put a hand on his chest. "I'm lighter. We have no idea how deep it is or how far it goes. If I get stuck or something happens, you'll have to pull me out. You're bigger and too heavy for me to pull out."

Backing up, he nodded, reluctantly conceding my point. "I still don't like the idea. You could get hurt." Hacking off a long, sturdy branch he handed it to me. "Use this to probe ahead of you."

Tapping the ground in front of me, I felt it get soggy and then turn to squishy mud. I stepped cautiously into the mud and squealed as I felt it soak through my shoes and between my toes. It was only ankle-deep at first, but as I approached the center, I sank to my knees. Pushing on, I was able to wade out the other side.

"Be careful," I told Mason. "I didn't feel any holes, but the mud is pretty thick, and it tries to suck you down." I grabbed some banana leaves and tried to wipe some of the sticky mess off my pant legs and shoes. "The stick helps with balance. You might want to cut one, too."

~

Bushwhacking through the jungle meant we progressed very slowly. Parachute material is super lightweight, so we'd brought quite a bit of it with us.

"I don't think I can walk anymore today, Mason, and it's going to be dark soon. I think we need to find a place to stay for the night."

"What will make you comfortable?" he asked. "There are no hotels around here."

"Well, I brought some stuff to make hammocks with. I really don't want to sleep on the ground. I don't like bugs, and

I especially don't like snakes. I have a feeling this jungle is crawling with both."

"Let's see what we come across. Nothing around here looks like a good place to call home for the night." Mason surveyed the thick jungle around us. "It's just more thickets, bushes, and scrub. Not even any sturdy trees."

We walked for another hour before Mason spotted a contender. "What about that?"

He'd found a giant chilamate tree. Its long roots provided lots of places to string up our makeshift hammocks. It was really just a rectangle of parachute material gathered and tied at each end with a length of parachute cord. The hammock would get us up off the ground, and a square of mesh tossed over the parachute cord ridgeline would, if we were lucky, keep most of the mosquitos away.

"Mason? What is that?" I asked, pointing to something moving in the bushes. A scaly triangular head could be seen at the front of a slithering length weaving through the leaves.

"Oh shit," Mason huffed out, stepping in front of me and putting out an arm to keep me back.

"Let me see, Mason. What is it?" I tried to elbow my way forward enough to see. I hate snakes, but I hated it more knowing there was one about but not where it was.

"Stay back, Kinsey. It's a giant snake." Mason was a rock, immovable. I wasn't going to get around him enough to see.

"I can see that. Is it leaving?" Craning my neck, I tried to see past him.

"No!" His voice boomed as he tried to push me further back so he could slowly back away. Then all hell broke loose.

Striking everywhere and in all directions, arcs of venom glittered through the air as the massive snake sprayed at everything that moved. The pale yellow liquid flew more than six feet all around it.

"Holy shit!" I gasped, eagerly tucking myself behind Mason as he hefted the crash axe in one hand.

"That's a fer-de-lance," he said, still backing away from the furious, writhing snake.

"A what?" My voice was shaking, and my limbs trembled.

"A pit viper. It's killed more humans than any other snake in the world. I've read about them but never seen one."

Suddenly lunging forward and swinging the axe at the approaching viper, Mason cut the head clean off. Rolling to the side, the severed head kept snapping and spitting venom.

"Mason, I don't want to stay here." I said, even though it was a perfect spot to hang our hammock. I couldn't even look in the direction of the twitching, dead snake.

MASON

I could tell Kinsey really didn't want to walk anymore, but she kept moving forward, glancing back over her shoulder as though we were being pursued. The snake encounter had really rattled her. I was just glad neither of us was hurt.

The fer-de-lance had been vicious, and we were lucky neither of us had been struck by the flying venom. The pale yellow liquid would have made our skin bubble had it struck us. That was an enormous snake, its body as thick around as my arm. If I'd missed with the ax, neither one of us would still be walking.

We started going downhill. The terrain was steeper, and the heat and humidity was sucking all the fluid from our bodies. We quickly blew through several bottles of water. Our supply was dwindling, and there were no fresh water sources in sight.

The muck pulled harder on my sneakers, making it more difficult to walk, and slowing us down. Kinsey didn't say a word. She followed in silence behind me.

As the day grew hotter, the mosquitos began attacking, getting their fill of blood from both of us.

"Come here." I stopped and pulled Kinsey toward me.

"Mmmph," she said, so tired she could barely speak.

Turning her around, I opened her pack and pulled out a short length of netting. I draped it over her head and tucked it into the collar of her shirt. "Here. This will help."

Nodding slightly, she resumed plodding down the trail. Trying to keep the thickets of thorns from slicing into her arms, she twisted and bent her body around the thick bush. Finally, she stopped before a series of fallen trees. There was no way to cross them. We were forced to crawl on all fours, to weave under and through them before we resumed our trek up the next ankle busting ridge.

The hours passed as we dipped and climbed higher into the jungle, the miles blurring into one unending trail of heat, humidity, muck and misery. Near the top of one ridge, we came to a small clearing. It offered no massive chilamate trees or anything big enough to tie our makeshift hammocks to, so we had to improvise. We piled banana leaves six inches high to make a mattress, and covered ourselves with the net.

"Mason, are you asleep?" Kinsey's voice flowed over me, pulling me from my reverie. I was lying there, picturing my Jacuzzi bathtub filled to the brim with hot, steamy water, and an ice bucket holding a chilled bottle of champagne. In my mind, I could see condensation dripping from the bottle and forming cold puddles on the edge of the tub.

"No," I ground out. Our banana leaf bed was not nearly as comfortable as the hot tub I had been imagining.

"What are we going to do?" She said in a small voice, rolling over toward me in a wasted attempt to get more comfortable.

Stars twinkled through the canopy above us and played peek-a-boo as the winds shifted the tops of the tallest trees. "We are going to keep going." Pausing, I thought about it. We had barely covered five miles. The terrain was so rough, the undergrowth so thick, we couldn't make any steady progress.

"We're almost out of water, Mason. We walked all day and are only a few miles from the plane. Even in the little bit we covered, we saw no signs of other humans anywhere." Flipping over on her back, she pulled the netting a little further over herself. The whine of mosquitos and the chirps of tree frogs served as haunting background music to the occasional mournful cry of a jaguar echoing through the night from a near distance.

"I don't know how, but we *will* make it out of here," I promised. "I refuse to die forgotten in some godforsaken jungle." I squeezed my eyes shut. "Tomorrow we'll get up and do it again. And we will do it every day until will figure out how to get out of here."

Chapter Seventeen

KINSEY

The clearing was just starting to lighten when I crawled out from under the net, shook out my shoes, and stumbled a short distance into the scrub to relieve myself.

Dropping my pants and squatting, I peed quickly. The mosquitos found my tender flesh and began feasting on my rear the instant it was exposed. You never realize how much you count on toilet paper and fresh water until you have to ration both. Two squares, that's all I allowed myself, and there was no fresh water to spare.

Standing and adjusting my clothes, I tucked my shirt into my pants and my pants into my socks. The fewer openings for things to crawl in, the better, I reasoned. Then I staggered back to our makeshift bed.

"Can we go?" I asked Mason, prodding him with a toe to rouse him.

"Yeah, we can go." He squinted into the dawn light. "Just as soon as I figure out how to make my body work again. Right now it's really mad at me and doesn't want to move."

"Hah! You're funny. Get moving, hot stuff." I yanked the

net off of him and folded it up to store in my bag. Packing away everything except a bottle of water and two granola bars, our morning food ration, I was ready and waiting to go while he was still rubbing the sleep from his eyes.

"Oh, shit!" Mason suddenly jumped to his feet and stumbled backward.

"What? What happened?" I exclaimed rushing to his side and running my hands up and down his limbs. "What hurts? Are you hurt?"

"Kins, I'm okay. I'm okay. I'm sorry. He just startled me."

"He? He who? Who's here?" I looked around, still not understanding.

"The black scorpion in my shoe," Mason said, capturing my hands in his and pulling me down to sit with him. "I shook my shoes out before putting them on and a big scorpion fell out. I really wasn't expecting it, but I'm okay."

Crying, I crumpled into him. The stress and strain of the crash and the uncertainty of our future washed over me. Wrapping his arms around me, he let me sob until I was cried out. Rubbing my back and making soothing noises, he rocked me as the fruit bats banked and dived above us, filling their bellies full of tasty mosquitos.

"I want to go home." Sniffling, I raised red-rimmed, tear-filled eyes to look at him.

"Me too. Kins. Me too." He wiped a knuckle across my cheek, catching a tear.

Sitting up and wiping my wet cheeks, I was suddenly done crying. A wave of determination washed over me. "Let's go. I want to get out of this godforsaken jungle as fast as we can."

"Alrighty then," Mason said, startled by the sudden change in my demeanor. Leaning my way, he used a thumb to rub something on my cheek. "You missed a spot. I think the rest of the dirt is on my shirt."

"Oh no!" I looked at his shirt and the smudgy wet mess I'd

left on the front of it. He was right; I had smeared dirt all over him.

Chuckling, he winked. "Now that's better. You have some color in your cheeks again." He shook out his shoes one last time before he slipped them on and stood. He helped me to my feet, and placing a quick kiss on my forehead first, he handed me my pack. "Let's go home."

MASON

That day was no easier. After an hour of walking, near-biblical rains began to fall, pounding through the trees and down onto us with unrelenting ferocity. It ran down my face, dripped off my nose, and soaked my clothes and shoes. What started as a shitty day became even shittier.

"Kinsey," I shouted over the roaring rain, "come over here." I gestured toward a banana tree with big leaves. It would provide some shelter until the storm passed. Huddling together, we crouched under the leaves and watched the rain fall.

"Mason!" Kinsey suddenly straightened, her eyes lighting up. "It's raining!"

"Yes, babe, it is raining."

"No, Mason, I mean it's raining! Fresh water!" She twisted and dug into her pack, pulling out several empty plastic water bottles. Wriggling out of the space we had tucked ourselves into, she held a bottle under the tip of a banana leaf, funneling precious fresh water into her bottle until it overflowed.

"You're a genius, Kinsey!" I couldn't believe I hadn't thought of it. In an instant she had solved one of our deadliest problems—our lack of water. We both filled every empty bottle we had, downing several and refilling them. We drank until we were satisfied and then drank some more.

After a few hours of staring into the rain, Kinsey announced, "I'm taking a shower." She proceeded to strip naked and step out into the monsoon, lifting her face to the sky and standing perfectly still like a marble goddess. She let the water course over every curve and dip of her body, running in rivulets down her skin and washing away the horrors of the last few days.

I couldn't stand it. She was too beautiful, and the events of the last few days had thrown us even closer together. The more time I spent with her, learning about her, the more attractive she became. Her mind and heart were just as beautiful as her drop-dead gorgeous packaging.

Shedding my clothes, I draped both hers and mine over nearby bushes to let nature rinse them clean. Then I stepped out into the rain with her. Placing my hands on either side of her face I leaned in, touched my lips to hers, and delighted in the warmth I found there. She opened her eyes and looked into mine. Then she leaned into the kiss, bringing her hands up to my shoulders.

After a moment, I pulled back and ran my hands from her face down to her shoulders and then down to her breasts. I tweaked the pebbling tips of her nipples, and they puckered tight in the cold rain. Wrapping my big hands around her rib cage right beneath her heaving breasts, I kissed her again. I laid a trail of kisses down her jaw, across her shoulders, and along her collarbone.

Her head fell back, and she gave in to the feeling, reveling in the heat of my mouth on her skin as my kisses trailed lower and lower to the short blonde curls at the apex of her thighs. Parting her nether lips I licked between them, searching for her pearl. I found it with my tongue and lapped at it, making her writhe in pleasure as the tension fell away. She was overcome with pleasure.

Easing her down to the wet earth, I hooked both her thighs over my shoulders. Little mewling noises escaped her, and she ran her fingers through my hair as I licked and sucked at her bud. Her legs trembled and locked around me.

"Oh my God, Mason. Oh my God!" Her voice rose with ecstasy as she cried my name. "I can't, I just…"

"Just let go, Kinsey," I said as I gently rubbed her bead with one finger. "Let yourself feel." I whispered, as I found her opening with my other hand. "Relax. Let it come."

Sliding first one finger, and then another into her slick opening, I began to ease them in and out, watching her lovely face as I resumed my oral adoration of her clitoris. I could feel swelling beneath my lips, throbbing at the tip of my tongue.

She grabbed my hair with both hand, forcing me deeper as her hips rocked to my rhythm. Her back arched and blond hair cascaded down off her shoulders. "I'm gonna come, Mason!" It was a warning and a cry for permission all at once.

"Let it happen," I said, drinking in the sight of her. "Come for me, Kinsey." I increasing the pressure on her button and plunged my fingers in and out of her even faster.

Suddenly, she was bucking against my mouth. Her inner muscles clenched around my fingers like a vice. She quivered as her orgasm flooded out of her, soaking my fingers and unshaven chin.

"Oooooh!" She threw her head back and moaned her release into the rain.

When she was done, she lay limp beneath me, delectable, wet and ready. I rolled her over onto her hands and knees and pulled her back toward me. Her ass was round and perfect in my hands. She folded her arms and rested her head on them, her back arching perfectly.

I took a moment to drink in the arousing sight before plunging into her from behind, my engorged cock spearing her, splitting her wet folds. I threw my head back and groaned at the feel of her velvet channel. Slamming in and out of her, my hips pumped from pure animal instinct. I couldn't think or control my body. My cock swelled thicker, harder than I'd thought possible. I was a slave to my lust for her.

Kinsey came alive under me. She pushed back, her hips meeting my every thrust. I could feel her channel begin to clench and spasm around my shaft as a second orgasm began to rise. A hot wave flooded out from her as she moaned loud, unrestrained into pounding rain. Our primal dance went on, our bodies moving perfectly in time with each other, our final release coming nearer. She threw her head back, and I grabbed a handful of her flaxen hair.

We came as one.

Chapter Eighteen

KINSEY

*D*awn again and we seemed no closer to the coast than the day before. I stretched, enjoying the weighty presence of Mason next to me. His bulk reminded me I was not alone. My body was still humming from the night before. My nipples tightened at the thought of his touch.

The jungle was coming to life around us and the air filled with exotic and frightening sounds. Sitting up, I realized I needed to relieve myself, and I wanted a shower badly. The beautiful memory of our encounter quickly faded.

Trudging east again, day after day, I was losing hope we would ever get out of the jungle. Mason and I didn't have enough food to hike forever. Even rationing, which we had done from the beginning, we were running low. We'd been hiking for a week and my energy was as limited as our supplies.

The sun directly beat down on us, and I stopped for a moment to pull out Ricardo's pilot hat. Setting it on top of my ratty hair, I enjoyed the shade it offered, but only for a moment. Immediately, the gnats flocked to the cool shadows it cast on my face.

"Stupid gnats." I waved my hands around, but it did little to discourage the bugs. Diving into my pack again, I pulled out the square of mesh fabric I'd been using as a bug net. I tossed it over my head and tucked the edges into the collar of my shirt as Mason had on the first day to block the bugs' assault on me and keep them out of my nose and mouth.

He had forged a few yards ahead of me, leaving me behind to admire the ridges of his muscular back beneath his sweat-soaked shirt. I was lost in hungry thoughts when he suddenly turned and ran back toward me, slipping and sliding on the wet leaves in a panic.

"Kinsey!" His voice was hushed, but his eyes were wide with fear. "Hide!"

"What are you talking about?" I asked, wrinkling my brow and turning my head to look around us. I bent down and picked up my pack, using my knee to prop it high enough for me to swing it onto my back.

"No! Get down! We can't let them see us!" Grabbing my arm, he pulled me into the brush. The branches snagged my clothes and pack, and a broken branch cut my arm as I stumbled into the brush behind him. Blood oozed and dripped with a *splat* onto the green leaves and decaying jungle floor.

"What is going on?" I demanded, trying to slow the bleeding with what had been my last clean shirt.

"Just ahead," he whispered, "beyond those trees is a guerilla camp." A bead of sweat trickled down from his hairline.

"There are no guerillas in Nicaragua!" I scoffed. Convinced he was just crazy, I allowed myself to stand up. "Nicaragua is one of the few peaceful Central American countries." Maybe he'd spent too much time in the sun.

"No, really. Follow me. Just be quiet." Creeping out of the bushes we'd hidden in, he retraced his steps, and I followed him through the trees. Peering around a large hardwood, I realized we were at the edge of a clearing. Then I stopped breathing.

Mason was right—we had stumbled across a guerilla camp. There really wasn't anything else it could be. Dotting the landscape was a smattering of lean-tos and huts with metal roofs constructed of roughly cut poles. Most were open sided and only tied together.

In front of one small shelter, a wicked-looking machine gun was mounted on a tripod. A large ammo belt feeding into the gun trailed over a nearby lean-to's railing.

"What the hell?" I gasped, startled at the sight, and almost tripping over my own feet.

"Shhhhh!" Mason pressed a finger against his lips, reminding me to be quiet. Putting his mouth right next to my ear he barely whispered, "We have to figure out how to go around them. We can't risk being seen."

I nodded rapidly, my breath growing quick and shallow as I motioned for him to lead the way. I risked a glance back over my shoulder; the site of that camp burned into my retinas. A dead pickup truck sat nearby, vines growing through its broken-out windows. The rubber tires were cracked and falling off the rusty rims. Tarps strung over rotted picnic tables flapped lazily in the breeze, creating a background of white noise that blended in with the constant jungle sounds.

Following the stream we had stumbled upon a few days earlier had led us right to the center of their camp. They had tossed a few logs over the moving water, creating a makeshift bridge. Once we made it around the camp, we would have to find that stream again. It was going to lead us out of this jungle. We couldn't lose it.

MASON

I'd heard rumors of armed groups operating in the northern mountainous jungles of Nicaragua, but I'd never really believed it. Almost 30 years had passed since the Iran-Contra scandal. Even though I was seeing the camp with my own eyes, I still couldn't believe the contras were active again. Were they paramilitary rebels? Tactical offshoots of the criminal gang the Maras? Whoever they were, they were poor and desperate, which made them very, very dangerous.

I could smell the nervous sweat pouring off me. It had a tangy, metallic odor that regular sweat from physical exertion doesn't carry. My shirt was soaked, clinging to my skin and chafing under my arms.

Our progress seemed to drag out. Time slowed to match our pace as we silently drifted from tree to tree around the perimeter of the camp. I was afraid to get too far away from it and risk losing our lifeline—the stream. It had not only provided us with direction but also lifesaving water. We'd run out of the bottled stuff the second day. Water is heavy, and while we took as much as we could carry, it didn't last long in the jungle's hot, humid climate. Neither of us was used to the heat or the intense work of hiking back to civilization. We required more liquid than normal to function. We couldn't afford to get sick.

Snap!

About halfway around the encampment, I motioned to Kinsey to stop. I'd heard something, but I didn't know what. Quietly, I slipped off my shoes and handed them to Kinsey. Lifting my right foot high, I balanced a moment before coming down on the outside ball of my right foot, slowly rolling to the inside ball. Lowering my heel and then my toes I gradually applied pressure. As kids, Mark and I played a lot of cowboys and Indians, and this was the best way I'd found to walk in complete silence. Of course, you have to pick your foot placement carefully and avoid stepping on anything that will break or crack. Staying in the shadows, I matched my movements to the dip and sway of the vegetation as a light breeze wove its way through the jungle.

Stealthily making my way through the brush, I tried to minimize the swish-swish sound my pants made. For an office guy, I was doing a pretty good job of remaining undetected. I'm sure the Army Rangers would laugh at my efforts, but I was doing the best I could in a pretty shitty situation. Then I made one wrong step and *CRACK!* Something broke beneath my bare foot.

Oh shit!

"¡Oye!" I had startled one of the guerrillas as he took a leak in the trees. Raising an alarm, the angry rebel fighter zipped his pants and gave chase. "Te voy a enseñar cuántos hoyos tiene un caite!" he shouted to the others.

Damn he's fast! The thorns and twigs cut my feet as I led him as far away from Kinsey as I could. Weaving through the vegetation, I dodged the low-hanging branches and vines that threatened to strangle me. Barely avoiding roots reaching up to trip me, I ran as far and as fast as I could until I could no longer hear the sounds of his pursuit. Then I leaned over, put my hands on my knees, and fought to catch my breath.

BANG!

BANG! BANG!

My heart stopped at the sound of gunshots echoing through the jungle. I stood up, frantically trying to identify the direction the shots had come from. *Where's Kinsey?!*

Taking off the in the direction I'd just come, I prayed I could find my way back to her in time. My fear for Kinsey fueled me even in my exhausted state. I couldn't bear the thought of anything happening to her. Ignoring the pain, I sprinted past the broken branches and overturned earth I had just left in my wake and raced back to the camp.

"Alto ahí! Stop there!" a sharp voice commanded. I froze with one foot in the air and slowly looked in the direction of the voice. "No te muevas! Don't move." A guerilla with a heavy accent gestured at me with his gun. I raised my hands, careful not to make any sudden moves, and turned to face him.

His chest puffed out and he swaggered over, resplendent in his dirty, tattered camos and a red bandana tied around one bicep. "They will shout my name tonight," he boasted. "I will be king when I tell the story of your capture!"

I watched him strut around in the clearing, crowing in his broken English as he told me what a big man he was to have captured me. His eyes darted back and forth as he licked his lips and pulled a walkie-talkie off his belt. He dropped the muzzle of the gun to the ground as he held the radio to his mouth, letting loose a string of Spanish I couldn't decipher.

Realizing it might be my only chance, I lunged at him, tackling him to the ground. The walkie-talkie flew from his hand. His rifle slipped from his shoulder and fell to the soft earth. We wrestled, rolling back and forth in the dirt. Mud and debris stuck to my sweaty skin and made it even harder to maintain a hold on my rebel captor. Spotting a rock out of the corner of my eye, I reached for it, but barely brushed it with my fingertips.

"I will keeel you!" the soldier hissed. His black eyes narrowed, and an evil sneer curled his lips, exposing his rotting teeth. Elbows and fists flew as we tumbled again, and I struggled to stay on top of him. Reaching for the rock again, I finally grasped it in my fist.

As he cursed and fought to throw me off, I brought the heavy rock down on his head. Instantly, his body went limp beneath me. Maybe I could have stopped, but I didn't. I lifted the rock high over his head and brought it down again and again. His skull made a horrible crunching sound until it caved, and then there was only the squishing sound of stone pulverizing tissue.

When I was certain he was dead, I stayed there for a

moment, studying my assailant's broken head as my adrenaline slowly faded away. Finally, my heart stopped racing and
my thoughts became clear. I rolled off of him, onto my back
and stared up at the sky peeking through the thick jungle
canopy.

How the hell did I get from my executive office to here?

KINSEY

H uddling down in a dense bramble thicket, I tucked
myself and both our packs as deep into the vegetation
as I could crawl. Bits of leaves and other detritus from the
forest floor clung to my clothes and hair, creeping into my
mouth and nose as I pressed my body into the damp earth.

I could hear shouting in Spanish and men running back
and forth. Their shadows fell over my hiding place. I was too
close to camp for comfort. All it would take was one eagle-
eyed, attentive rebel to spot me, and I'd be a dead woman. Or
worse.

Hunkering down, I squeezed my eyes shut and pictured
Mason's face. Regulating my breathing, I listened to the
movement around me. All the regular jungle sounds were
gone. No birds sang. No monkeys howled. Every creature had
fallen silent when chaos erupted. The ominous quiet terrified
me.

BANG!

BANG! BANG!

Shots sounded across the clearing, igniting a new and
furious commotion. *MASON!!!* I covered my mouth to stifle a
scream. I could hear the rebels shouting and see their shadows
rush across the leaves. I prayed that they hadn't found Mason
and, at the same time, that they wouldn't find me. I had to
figure out how to put space between me and them. I had to
find Mason.

Counting the seconds I squeezed my eyes shut again. *One, two, three…*

…two thousand, two hundred forty-nine… My eyes snapped open when I realized the jungle sounds were back and I hadn't heard voices in a while. Crawling an inch at a time from under the brush, dragging the two packs behind me, my senses were set on high alert. I crept away from the clearing, following the direction Mason and I had been traveling.

When I reached safer ground, where I was sure no one was watching, I stopped to adjust my load. Putting my own pack on my back, I tightened the straps and buckled the belt. Then I hoisted Mason's onto my front. We couldn't afford to lose anything, but I couldn't afford to let it slow me down, either.

Petrified, I kept moving in the direction Mason had been leading us. As frightened as I'd been throughout our entire trek, without Mason, I was almost too afraid to breathe. I prayed he was okay, that he'd figure out where I went and catch up to me. I just couldn't stay that close to the camp any longer, and I had no idea which way he'd gone. I hated to leave him behind, but I had to put some distance between me and the guys with the guns.

It took far longer than it should have for me to work myself the rest of the way around the camp and continue following the stream. It was easier walking along the water; the area was more open and clear of brush. Unfortunately, that also meant it would be easier for the rebels to find me.

I was thankful for the bright moonlight as I walked long into the night. I couldn't imagine making shelter without Mason, so I kept moving well past when we usually stopped. Staggering sometimes from the weight of the packs, my exhaustion gave way to numbness as I put one foot in front of the other over and over again.

Chapter Nineteen

MASON

I pulled two banana leaves from a tree and roughly fashioned them into shoe-shaped pieces. Holding them against my foot with one hand, I used the other to wrap them in place with the sleeves I'd torn from my shirt. It was little protection for my ruined feet, but it was at least something. Going barefoot might have kept me quiet and alive, but it exposed me to every twig, rock, and thorn on the jungle floor. At least the banana leaves served as a barrier as I set off to find Kinsey.

I don't know if it took me hours or mere minutes to make my back to where I thought I'd left her, but I was sweating buckets all the way. My heart hammered in my chest as I gingerly traced my route back, keeping an eye out for the guerrilla fighters.

My mad flight through the jungle was so unplanned and unorganized it took me a while to even find, much less follow, my random path back to the camp. I had to hide several times, avoiding the armed men who still combed the jungle in search of me. I couldn't risk getting caught. I had to find

Kinsey. She was all I could think about. *Did they find her? Is she okay?*

I caught sight of the guy I'd startled earlier when his pants were down. He looked seriously pissed. With his grenade launcher at the ready, he stalked through the jungle in his dark green uniform, sleeves rolled up in deference to the heat. I guess having to tell your boss you were surprised while taking a leak in the middle of nowhere wasn't good for job security. I bet it had earned him a sharp dressing down.

Searching through the thicket where I had left her, Kinsey was nowhere to be found. My heart tripped double-time as I circled wider and wider around the bushes. *I know this is where I left her!* Eventually, I stumbled across my shoes in the bushes, but there was no sign of Kinsey.

Wait? That looks odd. Kinsey had left my shoes lined up toe-to-heel pointing east. My eyes widened as I realized what she'd done. *God I love that woman!* Not only had she made the right decision to get the hell out of the hot zone, but she'd left me a message to let me know she'd gone east.

I unwrapped most of the fabric from around my raw feet and slipped my shoes on. The swelling was so bad I could only tie them loosely. Hobbling forward, exhausted, I ignored my aching feet and set off through the woods after Kinsey.

Hours later, the moon cast long dark shadows over the black and white landscape as I chased after Kinsey. Normally brightly lit and vibrant, the jungle seemed like a different place at night. Everything seemed malevolent, and my overactive imagination conjured danger around every corner. Moving cautiously around a bend in the river, I noticed how the stream widened as yet another branch joined it. The water was significantly deeper and faster in the middle than it had been when we'd started walking that morning.

Groaning, I stumbled to the bank. My eyes felt like sandpaper, and my feet hurt so badly I couldn't force myself take another step. I gently pulled my shoes off my poor feet and lowered them into the cool, soothing water.

"Ahhhhh." I couldn't stifle the sigh as the icy water provided instant relief. Leaning back on my elbows, I took a minute to enjoy the sensation before sitting up again and rinsing out my filthy shirt. I used the wet fabric to wipe off any exposed skin I could reach. My chest, neck, face and back—quite frankly all of me—was rank. I was covered in sweat, muck, and forest floor. I reveled in the blissful feeling, washing away the dirt and fear from the day.

"Mason?"

I jumped at the sound of her voice. My eyes widened, and my heart picked up speed. Hearing my name whispered in the moonlight raised gooseflesh on my already-chilled skin. My shoulders sagged with relief to see Kinsey's sultry form emerge from the shadows. I hadn't seen another human in hours, and those humans had all wanted to kill me. I was so tired I had inadvertently let my guard down. It was a slip that helped her find me, but I was lucky something more dangerous hadn't discovered me first.

"Thank God, Kinsey!" I leaped up on my sore feet, splashing water on my pants legs and abandoning my shirt where I'd left it drying on the rocks. Racing to her, the pain in my feet forgotten, I scooped her in a giant bear hug.

"I was afraid I would never see you again!" she cried. "Oh my God, Mason, don't leave me again!" Her voice wavered, thick with tears as she stood cocooned in my arms.

"I won't, baby. I won't. I'm here. I won't leave you ever again."

KINSEY

"Mason, we need to get going." I rolled over onto his chest and enjoyed the warmth radiating from him. I lowered my lips to his and with just one quick touch, a tingle shot through me. I felt a stirring below that had been absent in the fear of the last few days. What I wouldn't have given for a soft bed, room service, and hours to learn every inch of him. "Wake up, babe. We need to move." My voice was a whisper, my lips a hair's breadth from his. I could feel the electric pull of his mouth calling to mine.

Flipping me over, he spooned his body around mine, and we lay together on the blanket, cuddled together like two puppies. The night before, we hadn't gone too far beyond the tree line next to the river. Both of us had been too exhausted to hike on after the strain of getting separated and escaping the guerillas. It had been scary, and had left us both too physically drained to do much more than collapse in a heap as the day's adrenaline wore off.

Lying there in the dark, every muscle aching, my brain had refused to turn off. I had realized as I hiked alone that day that I could do this—I could get myself to the river alone. I just didn't want to.

Together, Mason and I were so much more than we were apart. Memories popped to the surface of my consciousness, flashbacks projected on the back of my eyelids, forcing me to relive everything that had happened since Ricardo announced the failure of the first engine. I could have faced those trials and survived on my own, but I was so grateful to have survived them with him.

"I'd much rather take you up on this delightful offer." Mason interrupted my deep reflections, his chest rumbling behind me, his hot breath on the back of my neck.

"Mason!" I reach back, playfully swatting whatever part I could reach. His length nestled into my backside, creating a surge of moisture between my legs. "I'm not offering anything! We need to go! We are still too close to that camp. I want to put a lot more miles between us and them." My brain didn't believe a word my lips were saying.

"Fine. I'll pretend I believe you." Chuckling, Mason rolled away and sat up, running a hand through his dark hair. After two weeks in the jungle, it had grown longer, curling on the ends that stopped just below his collar. Dirty and tangled as it was, the long hair made him even more ruggedly handsome. He'd lost the crisp cut he usually sported with his business attire, and the relaxed look suited him.

We made a great team, so breaking camp didn't take us long. We'd gotten into a rhythm; I'd roll up the blanket as Mason filled our water bottles, and we'd split a bag of peanuts as we put our shoes on. We could be up and on our way in under ten minutes. It seemed silly—we weren't facing deadlines, and there were no clocks or watches for miles—but every minute we walked was a minute closer to making it out of there.

I saw pain flash across his face as he slipped his shoes on, but he doesn't complain. I saw the shutters drop over his eyes, hiding his emotions, His face went flat. Always the macho man, he took the pain with a stoicism I could never pull off. The flesh on his feet was red, angry, and oozing from countless festering wounds. He needed more medical attention than I could provide with our meager supplies. Sighing, I looked away. There was nothing I could do about his feet.

Untying the bandage on my arm, I looked at my own injury and was pleased to see it scabbed over. It didn't look infected. Down at the edge of the water, I washed the blood out and wrapped my arm again.

"Why don't you lead today?" I knew his pace would be slower than mine. Our roles had reversed. He had been taking care of and protecting me since we'd left the plane, but it was my turn to care for him.

He looked at me but said nothing before he turned and

started picking his way along the riverbank, sticking to the softer soil and trying to avoid the rocks. I'm sure the rough terrain was killing him. He'd been quiet since that first exchange when I woke him. This experience had affected us both. I think it was changing us. I just hoped we were both changing for the better.

Once a care-free party-boy, interested only in making more money, this new Mason seemed much more serious, more grown-up. New lines had appeared on his face, and more gray streaked at his temples. I was sure I'd changed, too. I felt more confident. Just thinking about my father no longer made my blood pressure rise. And while I would have loved his blessing on my life, I no longer felt like I need it to be whole.

MASON

Lower and lower we descended, making slow but steady progress down the mountain to a valley. The river we followed slowed more the further we walked, flowing gracefully over large round rocks that mountain runoff had worn smooth over the years.

Every few hours, we stopped and I soaked my feet, rewrapping them with clean strips of fabric we rinsed and hung from our packs to dry for the next time we stopped. I think it helped keep them clean and reduce the swelling. The last thing we had time to do was stop walking, but those breaks were the only things that kept me going. We had to push on no matter how bad my feet hurt. We were down to the last few bags of peanuts from the plane, and neither of us had a clue how to hunt or fish.

We continued our descent down the mountain, and the air around us ripened with the briny scent of the ocean. The last two days we hadn't talked much. The reality was we might never make it out of the jungle. It had been almost three weeks with no sign of the sea or civilization. I knew it was there, though, and if we kept going in a straight line, we'd *have to* reach it eventually.

We'd been pushing hard since we'd escaped the guerillas and were running out of food. Kinsey was totally freaked out, and we were both worried about getting caught again. Who knew what else is hiding in the jungle with us.

"Mason, what happened back there?" Kinsey asked me again, but I didn't want to tell her. She didn't need to know the gory details.

"What do you mean?" I played dumb. I was so tired I didn't know what else to do.

"I mean, how did we get away?" Dropping her head to watch her feet as she walked, she said, "I really thought he was going to catch us. One moment I was running through the jungle, and I could practically feel him breathing down the back of my neck, I half expected to feel a bullet in my back at any second. Then, the next moment, he was gone." She lifted her eyes to me. "Just gone."

I didn't say anything. How do you explain killing someone? Even though it was in defense of us both—he was intent on killing me, and that would have left her all alone and in danger—I worried what she'd think. Would she look at me differently? Would she still want to be with me?

I had never done anything like that before, and I never wanted to do anything like that again. I felt dirty. Up to now, my life had been predictable. Boring, even. I had everything I ever wanted, and after growing up poor, that felt really good.

This, though, I hadn't been prepared for. Not the plane crash. Not Kinsey coming into my life. And not how far I was willing to go to protect her.

"I did what I had to do."

KINSEY

Weak and exhausted from days of traveling in the muggy 90-degree jungle, we didn't speak much. We picked our way along the river, putting one foot in front of the other, just trying to eat through the miles of tropical terrain that still stood between us and the safety of civilization. I drank cool river water as much to convince my empty belly it was full as to keep hydrated. I brushed my hand across my stomach, feeling its new concave shape. Even the strictest yoga regimens had never managed to eliminate the last bit of pudge there, but the jungle had.

I was just slipping into another bout of self-pity when something strange caught my eye up ahead in the water. "Mason! Is that a fish trap?" Squinting into the rising sun, I could see rocks damming the width of the river and funneling the deeper water into a bamboo fish cage. "It is! Mason, look!"

Suddenly reenergized, I splashed through the water and ran my hands across the cage. It was the most beautiful thing I had ever seen. "You know what this means?! This means people!"

He smiled and nodded wearily. "If there's fishing, we can't be too far from civilization. Lead the way." Mason gestured ahead as I steadied myself on a slippery rock and hopped back to the riverbank. "I'm ready for a hot shower and a juicy steak."

"Me too! And shampoo! I've been dreaming of shampoo, and body wash, and a hairbrush. Oh my God, I can't wait to run a brush through clean hair…" I got totally lost in the fantasy, I could almost feel the hot water coursing over my body, the warm drops hitting my face, running down my chest, over my breasts and pattering on the tile around my feet.

"Careful, Kinsey. Don't slip." Mason offered me a hand as

I crossed the last few rocks and headed downriver again, hiking with renewed vigor, my hope restored.

MASON

W hen we finally limped into the little fishing village four or five hours later, I was barely keeping up. I had started to think we had imagined the fish trap.

A dark-haired woman in a brightly colored skirt stared at us as we walked in with our soiled designer jeans and trendy sneakers, now all covered in mud and muck.

"Um, hi!" I tried to appear harmless as I approached her, but it was a struggle given how excited I was to see an unarmed person. "Can you help us, please?"

Hacking open tortoises for stew, she paused at our words, bloody machete in the air. She turned toward a hut in the distance and shouted, "José! José! Hay gringos!" Then she returned to her gruesome work, rendering the turtles to stewable chunks.

A short, stocky man in a dirty tank top and board shorts came from a small thatched building nearby, shack-rattling salsa music thumping from inside.

"Ah, hello?" He wiped his hands off on a greasy rag, "Can I help you?"

"Oh thank God. Can you help us, please?" I skidded to a stop in front of him, babbling some more. "We were in a plane. We crashed in the jungle. We've been walking for days."

"Ah... my English not so good... you like eat?" He led us to a ring of stumps around a central fire pit in the middle of the small village. It was really more a collection of a half-dozen primitive shacks than a village, maybe a family compound, but to my eyes, it was the most wonderful place in the world.

"My mother… she cook." The older woman we'd first met brought us two steaming coconut-shell bowls of some type of stew. I'm guessing it was tortoise. It was the most delicious food I'd ever eaten. The flavors exploded on my tongue. The tortoise was rich and meaty. The potatoes were soft and fluffy. The vegetables were full of life, and it all came together in a spectacular medley of flavors.

"Do you have a cell phone we could use?" I asked when José came back. "We really need to call home and let them know we're alive."

"Ah… no phone in village. Must go to Bilwi for phone."

"Bilwi?" Kinsey sat up and raised her eyebrows. "Where is Bilwi?"

"Bilwi… two day walk… down river."

I tried to stand, but stumbled. A low groan escaped me as I struggled to brace myself with one hand on a stump. Finally, I managed to right myself enough to wobble over to our packs.

"Man hurt?" José looked at Kinsey and waved at me as I slowly hobbled my way back to my stump.

"Yes," Kinsey said, her eyes damp with concern. "His feet are really bad."

"Feet?" He looked over his shoulder, "Mamá!" Then he turned to me. "Man show Mamá feet."

The old woman waddled over, shoulders stooped and bent at the waist. Her wizened face, deeply grooved by years of hard work and unrelenting sun, cracked a warm and gentle smile.

Still, I was worried. "I don't know," I said. "I'll be fine."

"You won't be fine, Mason. Show her your feet." Kinsey put her hands on my shoulders. "Please," she whispered.

I couldn't deny her anything. As I unwrapped my feet, the bandages stuck to the open wounds before painfully tearing away. The ragged strips were soaked pink with blood and green and yellow with pus. I could from the rotting odor that they were really bad.

The old woman leaned forward. I could almost hear her joints creaking as she bent to examine my injuries. She sniffed.

"Su pies apesta!" *[Your feet stink!]* She called out, shaking her finger at me. "Están malos." *[They are bad/infected.]* Tottering away, she went into a small mud and thatch hut.

"Where did she go?" Kinsey asked José. A moment later, the old woman was back, carrying a bowl in her hands. "What —what is THAT?" Kinsey's nose wrinkled and she backed away from the stench of whatever it was the old woman came out holding. "That is disgusting,"

She was right. I turned my head from the smell as bile rose in the back of my throat. It took all my self-control to hold back the gagging and resist the urge to throw up all the stew.

"Mamá fix feet," José said. "You sit."

Kinsey stood behind me, her hands massaging my shoulders as the old woman went to work. She pulled a sponge out and ran water over my feet, sponging them off and wiping away the dirt. With great care, she cleaned my wounds. When she was satisfied, she began scooping the green goop out of the bowl and painting it all over the raw flesh. With my feet completely covered, she bound them again in fresh strips of cloth.

"Wow." I was shocked at the instant relief. I could feel the lines in my face smoothing out as the pain in my feet faded away. "They don't hurt anymore. What is that stuff?"

Chapter Twenty

MASON

I may never know what was in that green goop, but the overnight difference in my feet was astonishing. The swelling was gone. The violent red signs of infection and inflammation were replaced with pink, healing flesh. The skin was still tender and would require a lot of babying to prevent reinjuring them, but I was well on my way to recovery.

José and his mother had given us a place to sleep and two more amazing meals. José was the only one in the village who spoke any English. With the rest, we did a lot of smiling and pointing. Kids ran up and touched Kinsey's blonde hair while the women giggled and hid. The men, except José, completely ignored us as they went about their lives.

We left a few things behind: some spare shirts, the extra parachute material and netting, anything we didn't think we'd need for the next two days. We were almost free of the jungle and had nothing else to thank them for their care and kindness with.

The riverbank widened as we neared the sea, and Kinsey and I walked shoulder to shoulder, quiet as morning dawned.

The sun rose and burned off the dew. Kinsey walked with her head high. She was thinner, her cheekbones more prominent, but it was the newfound confidence she exuded that captured my eye. God, she was beautiful.

Her hand swung by her side in rhythm with her step. I reached over, wrapping my hand around hers, enveloping her delicate fingers in mine. They fit perfectly as if they had always belonged together, connecting us.

We walked hand in hand from the shade of Mamá's shack into the swelteringly hot morning. There was less cover from the sun along the river than there had been in the heart of the jungle, and we both started sweating immediately.

Aside from the scorching sunlight, the river was beautiful. The bank was lined with flowers and fruit trees. Papaya, banana, and mango were all plentiful. They made for a tasty, if not terribly filling, breakfast and lunch.

"How long do you think it will take us to get to Bilwi?" Kinsey asked as she trotted along beside me, swinging our arms and periodically snuggling up as we walked. Her 1000-watt smile shined brighter than the sun. We both possessed a renewed lease on life knowing the city was so close.

"José said it was a two-day walk for him," I said, "but he's made the trek a hundred times. I think we should be prepared for it to take us three days." I grabbed my water bottle and took a swig, looking at Kinsey for confirmation.

"Ok. I can handle that." She took a deep breath. "Just think—in three days, this will all just be a memory."

"A memory that will live with us forever." I frowned, my lips pursing and my forehead wrinkling, "I keep thinking about Ricardo, Marie, and Matt."

"We can send someone back for them, right?" She looked up at me expectantly.

"I don't know, Kinsey. I plan to try, but I don't know if we could ever find that spot again. It's been almost three weeks.

By now the jungle will have claimed a lot of it. There might not be anything left to find."

We hiked quietly for a bit, the memory of the lost crew at the front of our minds. Then she asked, "Do you feel guilty?"

I didn't even have to think about it. "Yes. Every single day I ask myself, 'Why did we live when they died?'"

"I wonder that too. I just don't know, Mason." She sniffed and wiped beneath her eyes. "It doesn't make any sense."

"Growing up, I just wanted a place to call home. I thought if I could just make enough money to buy a house for my mom, that's all I would ever want. And then I made my first million and bought my mom a house, and then I thought, 'I just need a little more to be comfortable. This could all be gone tomorrow.'"

My heart hurt thinking of my mom and how she probably thought I was dead. I could picture her crying alone for hours. I thought about Mark, Laurie, and the twins—my family, which I'd ignored so often for work. *Will* they miss me? I missed them. In fact, I missed them more than my work. They were the reasons I had to live... and Kinsey.

"I feel like that now," she said. "The fights with my dad, boarding school, the car—it's all meaningless. All I want to do is live. This experience has shown me what's really impor-tant... and how quickly it can all slip away."

Stopping in the middle of the trail, I turned Kinsey to face me. My fingers wiped the sweaty hair from her face before my hands settled on her shoulders. I looked her straight in the eye. "Thank God I have you, Kinsey. You have kept me going through all this. I couldn't have done this without you. I never would have wanted these circumstances, but I have loved our time together." I paused. "I love you."

Her lovely blue eyes sparkled as a soft, pink smile spread across her sunburned face. "I love you too, Mason. If I had to be stranded after a plane crash in the jungle, I would only want it to be with you."

KINSEY

Cresting the hill after a strenuous climb through some challenging terrain, Mason and I were suddenly standing on the precipice of a cliff. The river reached the very edge of the ledge before falling hundreds of feet through the air and splashing into the turquoise pool below. The crystal clear water reflected the sky back at us, and in the shadows, we could see the depths of the basin hollowed out of the rock.

"Oh!" I gasped. My arms wind-milled, my heart fluttered, and my breath came in short bursts as I caught myself teetering on the edge of the drop off. Before I could fall, Mason's strong hand was on my shoulder, pulling me back from danger.

"Gotcha," he said.

I stared down the incredible height of the cliff wall. "How are we going to get down there?" Standing on the tips of my toes, I looked out over the wide open space, searching for a path to the bottom, but there was none.

"Careful, Kins." Mason said, extending a steady hand out to me. "We'll take it slow and easy. Follow me." Mason pulled the crash axe from his pack and began to swing at the thick brush that blocked our way. He cleared a rough, painful path through the scrub down the cliff face. It took hours. We were both scratched and bleeding by the time we reached the bottom.

A hot, tired and sweaty mess, I collapsed to the ground and yanked my pack off. I pulled the sticky fabric of my shirt away from my aching shoulders and massaged them for a moment before bending down and tugging off my shoes and socks. Padding barefoot to the edge of the turquoise pool, I plunged my feet into the cool water. *Holy cow!* The gorgeous waterfall was a lucky find, an oasis of calm beauty in a sea of chaotic jungle.

"Hey! Look what I found!" Mason's voice echoed from across the water. I could see him standing behind the waterfall and peering out from through the veil of water. "There's a cavern back here!" With a laugh, he dove through the falling river and off the ledge, into the dark depths below. He surfaced a moment later, spewing water and laughing as he swam over to where I sat.

"There is a big space behind the waterfall. Why don't we stop here for the night?" His face lit up, making him look about ten years younger. He hadn't smiled this much in days.

Playfully kicking my feet I splashed him, the cool water raining down over both of us. Squealing as I felt it land on my hot skin, I leaned back on my elbows and raised my face to the sun. "Alright, big guy. You set up camp behind the waterfall, and we'll stay. I want to clean up some." I sniffed my shoulder and scowled. "Ugh. It's been a week since it rained, and I feel gross. There's too much glorious fresh water here not to take advantage of it." I fell backward, lying flat on my back with my arms stretched out.

"Deal." He did a flip in the water and swam on his back before playfully rolling over and swimming back. Beside me, he hauled his gorgeous, dripping body out of the pool. "I'm gonna dry my clothes on that bush over there. Give me your pack and I'll take it with me."

"I've got it. You go on. I'll join you in a little bit." I had brought a tiny sliver of soap with me, and I fully intended to use it. While Mason set up camp behind the waterfall, I came to my feet and stepped into the water.

Standing fully clothed beneath the falling water, I soaped my hair, my body, my soiled shirt and pants, and let the water wash away the dirt. When it finally began running clear I pulled off my wets clothes and soaped up again, using my shirt to scrub every inch of my skin until it was pink and shiny. Then I stood there, shivering under the cold water.

In this remote jungle, far from everything I knew, I could see the beauty in its simplicity. I'd grown up with everything I'd needed, never having to worry about food, clothes, or shelter. In fact, I had more than I needed. It had never occurred to me that anyone grew up any differently.

College, work study, Mason, and the jungle had all altered my understanding of life. I was receiving both an education and a new perspective on the world. My life of opulence was a fantasy that had done nothing to prepare me for the real world. Dad cutting me off was probably one of the best things that ever happened to me. While I would love to have skipped the plane crash, even that horrible tragedy had taught me about myself.

The fishing village had been small, poor and very, very happy. You could see the love the mothers felt for their children, the husbands for their wives, and the children for their parents. Their lives were simple but full. They lived free of the unnecessary trappings of the modern world.

What little they had, the village had shared with us. The old woman nursed Mason. José's family fed us and gave us a place to sleep. They shared everything they had. My house was different, and Mason's even more so, when he'd had one before his father died.

I couldn't believe the side of him he'd shared with me. No one would ever guess Mason Alexander, playboy billionaire, had lived on the street, homeless and hungry. Who would suspect his dad had died penniless or that his mom had worked two jobs just to put food on the table.

Who was I compared to that?

What do I want out of life?

Chapter Twenty-One

MASON

*S*preading our clothes out in the sun, I took the time to empty our filthy packs. They'd been questionable to begin with, cobbled together from this and that, but after daily use and hundreds of jungle miles, they were stretched out of shape and wearing thin at the bottom. The hike had torn and spattered them with all matter of organic material. Sorting through their contents behind the waterfall, I shook out the two blankets we had with us, creating the best bed I could on the rock floor. The cavern was fairly shallow, but big enough for a king-size bed with space to the side for our bags.

I finished my chores and was ready to relax and have some fun. Cannonballing through the waterfall, I landed with a giant splash in the middle of the pool, sending a tidal wave of water over Kinsey as she floated blissfully on her back with her eyes closed, relaxing.

"Mason!" she squealed. She sat upright in the water and came after me. I pretended to run away, letting her catch me and laughing as she fought to shove my head under water.

Darting away I stayed just out of her reach, teasing her until I finally relented, letting her catch me again. "Got you!" she shouted in triumph as she wrapped her arms around my neck.

She was warm, wet, and naked. Catching me and sliding her body down mine until we were eye to eye, her playfulness suddenly changed. Her movements became sensual and fluid. Those delicate hands roamed my body, pushing me back until she had me pinned against a rock at the edge of the pool. They explored the planes of my back and chest, before venturing lower, following the trail of dark hair to the springy curls around the rod growing thicker and harder between my legs.

I closed my eyes and a shudder ran through me. She wrapped her fingers around my cock and began to slide her hand up and down the length of my shaft, stroking it from base to tip. Then her other hand cupped my balls, gently squeezing them, rolling them between her fingers as she leaned forward and kissed me. Her tongue explored the seam of my lips, dipped inside to tangle with mine, and then retreated before coming back to dance again. Our kisses deepened and I eagerly drowned in them.

"Sit on the edge," she whispered, her voice sultry, her eyes holding a promise of pleasure.

Boosting myself up out of the water, I did as she asked, watching her every move. My desire threatened to overwhelm me, and I started trembling as Kinsey advanced. Hips swayed as she rose out of the water, a goddess rising from the depths. She came to stand between my legs and knelt before me, taking the throbbing head of my rod into her warm mouth. Running her tongue around the tip, lightly stroking the crease, she sucked the rest of me into her mouth, until it touched the back of her throat.

Bobbing her head, her eyes crinkling at the corners, she looked up at me with a smile that said she knew exactly what she was doing to me. she slid up my growing length until only the tip remained in her mouth, then she plunged back down, burying her nose in the nest of curly dark hair encircling the base of my shaft.

Holding me in her mouth, gliding up and down the length of my shaft, her lips made a perfect rosy pink 'O' around me. She turned those big blue eyes on me once more and I was lost. I slipped into their depths and I let myself let go, cumming in waves, over and over again. She milked every last drop from me until I fell back, spent. I had no clue she could hold such power over me.

KINSEY

Curling up next to Mason, my head on his chest, a small satisfied smile played across my lips. This was the first chance I'd had to reciprocate the gift Mason had given me that day in the rain, and I thought I'd succeeded. Snuggling closer into his side, I wrapped an arm around him while he recovered. I could feel the aftershocks ripple through him as came down from his high. *I did that, I created that pleasure, and I have the power to do it again.*

Eventually, a hand came up to tuck me in closer to his side and caress up and down my arm. The light touch of his fingers caused the hairs on my arm to rise as goosebumps formed in the path they traveled.

"You are something else. I totally didn't expect that." The words rumbled through his chest as it rose and fell rhythmically below my ear.

"Sometimes a girl just has to exert her power," I said, giggling and propping myself up on my elbow. "I just didn't want to show my hand too soon." I started tracing circles on his chest.

"You definitely have the power." His smile glowed in the sunlight. "I don't think I can move."

"You mean you aren't going to take advantage of this naked woman in your arms?" I purred in his ear. "Really?"

"You gotta give me a minute. A man needs a little time to recover from something like that."

Chapter Twenty-Two

KINSEY

*M*ason refused to explain how we'd escaped the rebels. I was afraid I knew what had happened, but I didn't press him further. He didn't want to talk about it, and I didn't want to force him. Slowing down, I linked my arm with his and leaned into his strength as we walked.

"What is the first thing you want to do when we get out of here?" I asked, changing the subject to lighten the mood. Eventually, we would have to talk about all of this, but clearly now wasn't the time.

"Mmmm." Playing along he kissed the side of my head. "I want a steak—a juicy, cooked-to-perfection, oozing-with-flavor, thick porterhouse steak and a bottle of my best wine." He smacked his lips. "I can practically taste it. You?"

"A shower. A hot shower—no, wait—a bath. A long bubble bath. I want my strawberry scented bath gel, lots of frothy white bubbles, candles, soft music, and at least an hour of soothing hot water. I hurt all over. My bruises have bruises. Maybe a nice glass of cold wine, but mostly I just want hot water."

We settled our pace into a rhythm. The walking was a lot easier than it had been in the mountains. As we walked farther, the jungle thinned.

"Garbage!" Unlinking my arm, I reached down and picked up a plastic water bottle. "There was someone here!" Ever the optimist, I chose to think it was someone good. Finally we were starting to see signs of humanity. Looking ahead, I could see other bits of trash, and I knew we had to be getting close.

"Following the river, we *had* to hit the sea eventually. Maybe this is finally it." Mason looked relieved, his face losing the pinched expression he'd been wearing since he woke up from the crash. The lines in his forehead didn't seem as deep, and his eyes had a bit more life to them.

Coming around a bend in the river, I stopped. I couldn't believe my eyes. "Look!" I shouted and started running, streaking toward a small house that suddenly appeared like a mirage next to the water. Only, it was real.

The small shack had a clothes line strung up with shirts and pants flapping in the breeze. A small dog roamed the length of a chain in the front yard, yipping to announce our arrival. In a downstairs window, a curtain was pulled aside, and a face peered out at us.

We had made it.

MASON

The small house belonged to a poor Nica family. The father was a fisherman who made his living on the river. They spoke a native dialect, but the oldest child spoke enough Spanish and English to give us directions to Bilwi. This family was completely off the grid, but Bilwi was home to 30,000 people in Puerto Cabeza. One of them was bound to have phone service. We might even find an airport.

It was only a few more hours to Bilwi, and we practically ran the whole way. The sight of a telephone pole brought tears to my eyes. It was the first sure sign that we were definitely going to survive the horrible ordeal.

That first phone call was weird. Standing in the town square, an old fashioned pay phone was as close to modern living as the town had to offer. It was enough. Dropping in the coins I'd traded my extra shirts for, I dialed the international extension for the US and called Mark.

"Mason?!" I pulled the receiver away from my ear as he shouted. "Oh my God everybody, it's Mason!!!!" I could hear a chorus of cheers over the phone line. "Mason, is it really you? Don't go away! Where are you? Are you okay?" The questions came so fast they overwhelmed me.

"Yeah, yeah, we're fine. We're in Bilwi." I was surprised by my own lack of enthusiasm. It was almost a letdown, after the weeks of trying to find our way out of the jungle, to finally be there, safe.

"Where the hell is Bilwi?"

"We're on the east coast of Nicaragua. There's a little airport here. I'll explain everything later. Can you get us a charter into Managua?"

"Oh my God, yes! Anything! I'll set it up right now." I could hear him typing in the background. "We thought you were dead. Mom hasn't stopped crying since your plane disappeared. I was planning your funeral!!!"

"I'm not sure how we survived." I took a deep breath. "It's just me and Kinsey. The crew didn't make it."

Silence flowed over the line.

"I need to get some money, too," I said. "This is not a town that takes credit cards." My brain didn't want to switch over from survival mode.

"I am so sorry, Mason." Mark swallowed before continuing. "Don't worry. We're coming to get you. We'll be in Managua in six hours."

"Thank God, Mark. I can't wait to see you."

"I called Liam," he said. "I thought maybe he could help. He came back from God knows were. He's been trying to track the plane. He called in a favor at the Pentagon. The US military has been searching satellite images for the crash. Liam was ready to deploy his team to search the jungle on foot."

DO-DO-DO the phone trilled in my ear, *to continue your call, please deposit more money.*

"Mark, I'm running out of coins."

"I'm still working on a flight from Bilwi for you. Give me the pay phone number. I'll call you back in 15 minutes. Hang in there, Mason. It's almost over."

"Thanks, Mark." I hung the phone up and stepped back out of the booth.

Liam? He called Liam? I never thought I'd hear that name again. That angry kid had fought against everything Noah tried to do for the group of us. He'd enlisted in the military before he even graduated from high school, and on graduation day, he walked off the stage and out of our lives. I'd heard he was a spook somewhere for the CIA. I had no idea Mark was still in touch.

Mark wasted no time arranging the private charter. The air taxi flew from Managua to Bilwi, and we were strapped in for takeoff in under two hours. It was the only plane at the airport, the daily commuter having already left, so there was no waiting on the tarmac. We were in the air within minutes of boarding. An hour later, we were standing safely on solid ground again in Managua.

I was worried how we'd both do, our first time on a plane since the crash. I admit I was a little hesitant as I climbed in. The plane was old, the paint scratched and faded, but the pilot was an ex-pat, and after quick conversation about his military flight training, I trusted him.

Kinsey trusted me. "He's well trained," I told her as I helped her with her seatbelt. "The skies are clear." I took her hand in mine to reassure her, and that now-familiar tingle ran up my arm. When we hit some mild turbulence along the way, she whimpered and turned her frightened eyes to me. I brought her hand to my lips and kissed it softly, watching the tension drain from her face. I held her hand all the way to Managua.

A car was waiting for us when we reached our destination. The Aeropuerto Internacional Augusto C. Sandino, Managua's international airport, was busier than Bilwi's, and the sudden immersion into hustling, bustling civilization rattled me. Settling into the plush seats of the black Lincoln, I felt like an imposter. Unbathed in ratty clothes, I was not the Mason Alexander who took this all for granted. I was changed. As I wondered if Kinsey felt the same, I saw her shiver in the cold air conditioning, so I pulled her close and held her to keep her warm.

Chapter Twenty-Three

KINSEY

$\mathcal{I}$ think I was in shock. The last few hours flew by in a blur. From the moment I knocked on the door to the little house, to the moment we climbed into the limo, life sped by at a surreal pace. Shivering in the back of the limo, I snuggled close to Mason, the one constant in my life.

From the moment we boarded the plane in Bilwi until the moment the black limousine delivered us to the Hilton Princess Managua, I didn't speak. Something about the concrete lions that greeted us outside the hotel's glass entrance and the wall-to-wall marble in the lobby felt absurdly indulgent. We were back in the modern world of luxury and accommodation, but I seemed to have left my voice somewhere in the jungles of Nicaragua.

Alerted to our arrival, a concierge whisked us up to the executive floor and into a suite where 250-thread-count sheets, fluffy bathrobes, and a big bathtub awaited us.

Standing in the middle of the room, slowly turning in a circle, Mason saw my confusion. "Kinsey," he said, "baby, it's okay." He took me by the hand and led me into the bathroom.

Undressing me like a child, he spoke softly to put me at ease. He turned on the hot water and added some of the complimentary bath gel the hotel had left for us. "Here." He picked me up and gently set me in the tub. "Just close your eyes and relax, I'll be right back."

I don't know how long he was gone, but it was long enough for me to fall asleep. Waking as he returned, I realized the water had grown cold. Much of my stiffness was gone, my head felt clearer, and my stress was nearly gone. The bath had done its job.

At some point, Mason must have showered. He was clean and dressed in new clothes. He had shaved, and the whiskers that had graced his jaw for the past few weeks were gone. He looked younger, stronger.

Kneeling by the edge of the bath, he turned the faucet to hot, warming the cooling water. He took a soft washcloth from beside the tub and began to wash me. Slowly dragging a cloth along my limbs, he gently wiped away the dirt and grime until all traces of the jungle were gone.

Closing my eyes I fell into the sensation—the rhythmic swipe of terry cloth, the drops of water rolling across my skin, and the chill I felt when he withdrew his touch.

Moistening my lips, I became hyper-aware of my body. Every inch of my skin felt electrified with little jolts shooting through me wherever his hands landed. Tilting my head back, Mason poured warm water over my hair, massaged the shampoo through my blonde strands, and then rinsed away the dirt and oil.

Finally, he pulled the plug and the dirty brown water swirled down the drain. Mason lifted me out, wrapped me in a warm plush towel, and carried me into the bedroom.

Lovingly laying me on the bed, he rolled me onto my stomach. Starting at my shoulders, he began massaging my back, kneading the muscles, and working out any lingering tension.

"Kinsey, love, we did it. We made it."

Turning my head, I looked into his eyes, "We made it, but what about the others." My voice choked with tears, and I turned back, burying my face in the sheets. Shaking all over, I let out an uncontrollable sob. Rolling onto my back and sitting up, I waved Mason away.

I rested a shaky hand on my forehead and slid off the bed. I couldn't take it anymore, I got up and ran. I didn't know where I was going, but I just had to get away.

My legs still sore and my gait unsteady, he caught me before I even reached the door and pulled me close until my cries were buried in his broad chest. Wrapping his muscled arms around me, he held me there until I stopped shaking.

Gently rubbing circles on my back, he crooned, "It's all right. It's over. You're ok. You're safe now." As we stood there in the middle of the suite, he rocked me, swaying back and forth, and soothed me until my sobs subsided to whimpers, and my whimpers slowed into the occasional hiccup.

Suddenly the mood changed. The room felt warmer. The air turned from friendly and consoling to something... more.

MASON

Kinsey tilted her head back and looked up at me. Her big blue eyes were teary and pleading. Those soft, pouty lips parted as she exhaled. Every inch of her begged for my kiss.

The touch of her warm, naked body, still damp from her bath, was too much. I pulled her closer. My growing hardness nestled perfectly in the cleft of her legs. With one hand cupping the curve of her ass and the other holding her against me, I lifted her and carried her back to the tangled sheets. We didn't speak as our bodies came together again, a perfect fit, as if we were meant to be one.

Later, lying in a sexual stupor, Kinsey's head on my chest and her fingers playing in my chest hair, I wondered if what we had was real. Were my feelings the result of the plane crash? Was I confusing forced togetherness for love?

The real world was intruding, and our time alone together was coming to a close.

Have I made a terrible mistake? Noah was my friend and mentor. Kinsey was my employee. I never should have crossed that line.

Throwing back the covers, I stood and walked to the window. Standing there, looking out at Managua, I recalled the many times I'd stood just that way, looking out over New York City.

Ring... Ring...

Picking up the phone before it could disturb her sleep, I whispered into the receiver. "Hello?"

"This is Carlos at the front desk," a man said. "Some newly arrived guests are asking for you."

"Oh, yes." I'd forgotten our friends and family were on their way. "Please tell them I'll be right down."

"I will, sir, but..." his chuckled nervously, "there is a Mr. Noah Hendrix who is most insistent we allow him to come up. Could you please come speak to him? He's causing quite the commotion."

~

The clothes I'd had the concierge send up when we arrived felt uncomfortable. It was the first time I'd worn a suit in weeks. The collar felt too tight even though it was my standard size, and I could see in the mirror how loosely the outfit hung on my gaunt frame. I didn't have a scale, but I knew I'd easily shed 20 pounds trekking through the jungle.

Tugging my shirt cuffs to the perfect length beyond my coat sleeve, I inserted a new set of cufflinks and reached up to straighten my tie one more time. I wrote a quick note for Kinsey and left it on the nightstand next to her. With a kiss on her forehead, I tucked the blankets more securely around her. She was sleeping so serenely I didn't have the heart to wake her. It was her first peaceful sleep in weeks, and she needed it. Alone, I left to greet our families.

As I exited the elevator, I was overwhelmed by the crowd that rushed to greet me. Holding up a hand to stop the onslaught, I cautioned everyone to calm down. "Woah, woah! Everybody, calm down. Back up."

"Mason, I can't believe it's you!" my mother cried. Ignoring my plea for space, she enveloped me in a giant hug, or as giant as it could be from a 5'2" woman hugging a 6'5" man.

"Mom, I love you. Yes, it's me and yes, I'm fine." Patting her back, I tried to move us away from the elevators, but I didn't get far before Mark came for his turn at me.

"Where is my daughter?" Noah interjected, squeezing between me and my family.

"She will be down in a moment, Noah. She needed a little more time to compose herself. These last few weeks have been hard on her." I shook his hand with my right and gave him a man's hug with my left arm before turning back to my clamoring relatives.

Mark was there in an instant. He pounded me on the back with one hand while the other juggled a twin. He couldn't stop talking. "It's so good to see you. I can't believe you're here. Here," he said, passing me the baby, "hold Lily." I took the baby, and Mark's wife moved close to give me a neck hug. I was never going to make it across the lobby.

Giving up, I held up the one hand not holding an infant. "Everyone! Everyone! Guys, I love you all, but we've got to move this reunion somewhere else. Let's go get a table in the restaurant. I made a reservation when I got here."

I think my volume finally got through to them. Holding

Lily, my mother glued to my side, our procession made its way into the restaurant. The maître d' wisely seated us in an empty room.

It took a while, but I got most of the story out. While I spoke, the table fell silent. They all sat there, staring at me. "And that's the all of it," I said when I was done. Then the questions started again, a relentless train of curiosity broken only by Kinsey's arrival.

Noah stood and pulled out a chair for her, suddenly the solicitous father. Of course, he seated her at his side, far away from me. The protective father had come out. I don't know what I was expecting, but the distance he put between us cut like a knife.

His behavior reminded me why we couldn't be together. *I'm Noah's protégé. Kinsey is his daughter. He will never let us be anything to each other.*

From the far end of the table, Kinsey tried to talk to me, but Noah cut her off every time. "Were you able to find out about the China factor—"

"Don't worry about that now, Kinsey," he ordered. "Just take care of yourself and let Mason will deal with his business."

KINSEY

"Listen, Kinsey." Mason pulled me aside as we left the dining room. "Your dad is getting you your own room. Now that you have family here, he thinks you should be with him."

Opening my mouth to protest he placed a finger on my lips to quiet me. There was an odd distance in his eyes that I hadn't seen in weeks. "Don't worry. I explained how anxious you were about being alone when we got here, so he doesn't think we were sharing a room to sleep together. I told him I'd been planning to sleep on the couch."

Blinking, I just started at him, stunned. He'd just dismissed our relationship as a kindness to ease my anxiety. Was that all it was? Had I imagined every loving caress? *Was his declaration of love just a favor?*

"Kinsey…" He paused as if changing his mind about what he was going to say. Then, straightening his spine, he continued. "I'm so sorry, but this thing between us. It isn't going to work." Scrubbing his hand over his face he kept apologizing. "Ahhh, God. Kinsey, this is so hard."

I couldn't speak.

His face twisted in pain, he whispered, "Please forgive me. I knew Noah wouldn't accept this. I'm not good enough for you." He stepped back, putting a distance between us that extended far beyond any physical space. He severed our connection. It crushed me, making this return to civilization even harder than it already was.

I don't know if my father knew what was going on, but suddenly he was between Mason and me. "I'll come up and get Kinsey's things," he told Mason. "Kinsey," he faced to me, "here is your room key. Go ahead upstairs. I will be there to help you settle in once I collect your things."

"I don't have anything," I said. Taking the key, I turned and walked away. There was nothing in that room I wanted anymore.

Lying alone in my sterile hotel bed, the 250-thread-count sheets felt scratchy. The hum of the air conditioner was irritating, and every voice in the hallway grated on my nerves. *Why did we come back?* As awful as the jungle was, at least we were together there. *Maybe I did imagine it.*

Rolling over, I automatically moved to snuggle next to Mason and then had to remind my traitorous body that he wasn't there. I really did feel alone, bereft. My father, in the room on the other side of the connecting door, was no comfort to me.

"What changed, Mason?" I asked the empty room.

The year is really starting to suck. First I make headlines. Then Jason runs up my credit card bills and dad flips out. When Mason offered me a job, I thought things were looking up, but if this is the result, I would have been better off bussing tables and cleaning trash cans.

I believed him when he said he loved me. Now I wished we'd never run into each other that day in my father's lobby.

My heart hurt.

Chapter Twenty-Four

KINSEY

Slouching against the bulkhead in first class, I stared vacantly out the window of the jumbo jet taking me back to New York. Leaving Nicaragua, I felt like I was leaving behind a life I had only just glimpsed. I hated being on a plane again, but at least this one was a jumbo jet—huge compared to Mason's tiny tin can.

"Would you care for something to drink?" The stewardess with her beverage cart stood smiling expectantly. She reminded me so much of Marie I could feel the tears welling behind my eyes.

"No, thank you," I whispered. Turning back to the window, I stared out at the nothingness of bright white clouds stretching to the horizon.

I sat silently by my father's side for the rest of the trip. He must have felt my anguish because he remained mute for the entire flight.

I felt like my heart had been ripped from my chest. The physical reminders of the crash, the scrapes, bruises, weight loss, and exposure—all those would fade with time. I had no idea how to put my heart back together after Mason had smashed it to pieces.

~

I emailed Peter and asked for his father's contact information. Then, making a quick phone call, I feigned happiness and chatted gaily with Ambassador Zao. Mason may have been done with me, but I wasn't done with our work.

It was nice to catch up with the ambassador. I hadn't seen him in several years. We always seemed to miss each other at my father's events. I explained the problems Mason was having with the factory in China, and called in a favor. The ambassador agreed to visit the factory on his next trip and to work with the local representatives to solve the production problem.

"He should be back up and running at full capacity within a week," the ambassador said. "Tell your boss he will meet his deadlines." I thanked him and told him how I hoped to see him soon.

Before working at Mason's company and the subsequent crash, I never would have had the confidence to call Ambassador Zao. But I was a different person now. And this was business. One thing I had learned was that business was built on connections, and raised as I was, I had connections. It was time I learned to use them.

~

R eturning to college in the fall was bittersweet. I had one semester left at Columbia before graduation, and I was getting everything I wanted. I went through the motions, working in the lab, completing my assignments, smiling and chatting, but nothing felt real. There was a gray cloud over life.

I wanted to keep working and insisted on it, much to Dad's chagrin. To appease me, he had called in a favor with another of his protégés, Damon, and found me a new job.

Damon owned an energy company in Miami that had a small satellite office in New York. I wasn't exactly working in the BioTech field, but focusing on the business side of things meant I was still learning a lot. More importantly, it kept me busy. The last thing I wanted was time to think.

"Kinsey, have you seen my notes on the Synergy merger?" Damon asked, walking into the office.

"No. Sorry, Damon. Did you take them home with you last night?"

"Probably." He sighed, slumping at the shoulders and running his fingers through his hair. "They're fighting the buyout hard. I've got to go talk to the owners again and get them to calm their employees down. I don't know why they're fighting so hard. They'll never survive the way things are going."

I nodded. "Let me know if there is anything I can do to help." I said, looking at him with a critical eye. Damon was gorgeous with deep brown eyes, curly brown hair, and a chiseled physique. *I should feel something.* He was my type, but my heart just couldn't get past Mason. He was the only man I thought of. Even presented with a virile specimen like Damon, I could feel nothing for anyone else.

I was empty.

Chapter Twenty-Five

MASON

Sitting alone in my condo, back in New York, I booted up the new laptop Mark brought for me in Nicaragua and logged in to the Phantomfire Media servers. Encrypting my signal, I accessed the secure areas and started working. It didn't give me the same satisfaction it used to, though.

I was lonely. I missed Kinsey.

Noah would never forgive me if he found out about us. I couldn't believe I'd made love to Kinsey, and I couldn't believe I would never get to again. She was like a drug I couldn't get out of my system.

My eyebrows flew up, eyes widening as I read an email from the Ambassador to China. I had no idea how he found me or how he knew about the situation. He said he would be in Beijing and wanted to know if I would like to join him for a sit-down meeting with the local authorities and factory representatives. The fantastic news made my heart race for a moment, but then it stilled again.

I should be happy. Business was booming. In addition to the email from the ambassador, there were four more contacts inquiring about our chip. I had almost everything I'd ever wanted. What I didn't have could never be mine.

It didn't matter. I didn't have time for love, anyhow. While I was gone, Mary had returned to work, and my calendar was full. I added in the new meeting requests, and blocked out time to return to China with the ambassador. Still, it wasn't enough to keep her out of my thoughts.

I knew what Kinsey and I had wasn't real, but I missed it. I missed her closeness, her laugh, her wit. I missed the chess games in my office after hours. A relationship isn't something I'd ever wanted, but now that it was gone, it left a hole. She'd chosen Noah and college, a path I wasn't on. I chose Phantomfire Media. Our lives were not compatible. It was a fluke that we'd met again.

Now that she had patched things up with her father, she didn't need me anymore.

~

Time passed. Grief and pain became my constant companions. I lost even more weight and moved lethargically. I made excuses, turning down every offer from Noah to play racquetball, and locked myself in my office when I was at work. Ignoring phone calls from my family, dark circles settled under my eyes, and instead of sleeping, which I couldn't do anyway, I worked online long into the night.

Our stock was off the charts.

~

BANG!
BANG!
BANG!

Jumping up from my chair, I knocked over the empty glass sitting by my right hand. I gazed around my study, realizing I had once again passed out while working. A puddle of drool defaced my keyboard, and running my hand over my face, I realized I had a keyboard shaped imprint on my cheek.

"I'm coming, I'm coming," I hollered at the closed front door. The person on the other side was still hammering to come in.

I threw the door open, and Mark practically fell in, his hand still raised to bang again.

"It's about time! Where the hell have you been, Mason?" he said, striding in and squinting at the mess.

"I gave the cleaning lady a month off," I told him. "I didn't want to be bothered by anyone." I shot him a resentful glare.

"Why's that?" he asked, still taking in the magnitude of my housekeeping disaster.

"I've been busy."

"Too busy to call Mom back? She thought she lost you when your plane went down. She's a little fragile right now. Cut her some slack and call her back so she knows you're still alive."

"Yeah… okay." My voice was flat and I barely looked at him. Running my fingers through my hair, I was surprised how tangled it was. Haircuts were another thing I didn't want to be bothered by.

"She expects you at dinner tonight."

"Tonight? What's tonight?" Squinting at Mark, my brain was still foggy. I had no idea what he was talking about.

"Mom's birthday dinner? You told Laurie you were coming last week."

Sweating, I looked around the front room as if I'd find an

excuse not to attend hiding behind the couch. I really didn't want to see people, especially not family. They could see right through the bravado I projected at the office, and I couldn't stand to be exposed like that.

"Go. Shower. You stink." Mark scowled. "I don't know how Mary puts up with you. I'll wait right here until you're ready. Then you're riding with me to the party. You aren't getting out of this one."

Dragging my feet, I petulantly did as Mark ordered. I knew he was right that I needed to snap out of it, but I was almost enjoying my reclusiveness. I wasn't ready to stop licking my wounds.

"I mean it, Mason. It's been almost six months. Christmas is in a few weeks. You will come, and you will have fun." Mark called after me from the living room. "If I don't hear the shower running in five minutes, I'll come stuff you in it myself!"

"Fine!" I shouted back. "I heard you. Now mind your own business. I'll be out in a few minutes." There were times when I could do without an older brother. This was one of them.

"**M**ason!" My tiny mother swooped down upon me as soon as I walked in the door. "You came!" Trapping me in a hug, her perfume took me back to my childhood, when she would patch up my cuts and scrapes, always ending each emergency with her healing embrace.

Moving further into Mark's house, I stopped mid-stride when I spotted the twins. They were walking and babbling! Toddling back and forth on unsteady legs, one then the other would sit suddenly, crawl a few feet and then stand back up to toddle off again. Grabbing and bracing themselves on the many available adult legs surrounding them, they ran laps around the room. Squeezing my eyes shut, I shook my head. They couldn't possibly be walking already! Just six months ago they were babies asleep in Mark's arms in a hotel in Nicaragua.

Have I lost six months of my life?

Chapter Twenty-Six

MASON

Slicing open the light blue envelope, I pulled free the cream colored card.

"Please join us as we celebrate the graduation of Kinsey Bryce Hendrix from Columbia University on December 22nd at 5:00 in the afternoon."

Slipping through my fingers, the card fell to the floor. I couldn't breathe. It took all my focus to calm myself and suck in air.

There was no return address, no indication that the invitation was from Kinsey. I'd worked hard to relegate her to a part of my life that was over. She needed to be her own person, to grow into who I knew she could be without me holding her back.

I'd been so afraid that claiming her as mine would keep her from her dreams.

Maybe I was wrong. Maybe this meant something. Maybe she sent it to me for a reason.

Maybe this is a sign.

S itting in back of the auditorium, I opened my program and found her name. I was thrilled to see she was graduating with honors, magna cum laude in the top 3 percent of her class. She had done well, worked hard, and I was proud of her.

The problem was I missed her. I missed her smile and the way her bright blue eyes lit up when she was excited. I missed the way the bright blue turned indigo with desire. The curve of her back, the arch of her feet, the way the weight of her breasts in my hands—I wanted it back. I wanted her back more than I wanted anything.

"Kinsey Bryce Hendrix," the announcer read.

Watching her walk across the stage and accept her diploma, my chest filled with pride. She was finally getting the recognition for her brains that she'd craved for years. I leaned forward, my smile slowly growing wider as I watched the fluid way she moved. I sensed my heart beating in my chest, and the hair on my arms stood up straight.

She was so close and yet so far. I wanted to feel her, touch her skin, smell that uniquely Kinsey scent.

Jasmine. She smelled like Jasmine.

Interrupting my reverie, Noah was suddenly looming over me.

"Why are you here?" he spat out. "Haven't you done enough?"

I guess those invitations to play racquetball were an excuse to get me out and give me a piece of his mind. That would have been something he needed to do face to face.

Fumbling with my words, I didn't know what to say. *Why am I here?*

"You need to leave. Now," he said. "It's taken her months to get over whatever happened in the jungle. She won't talk about it, but I know you were part of the problem. Seeing you will set her back."

"I don't want to upset her," I said, deflating. I hung my head, my excitement for her achievements evaporating. "I'll go."

I could feel Noah's eyes boring into the back of my head as I walked up the aisle, away from Kinsey and any future we might have had together.

Chapter Twenty-Seven

KINSEY

$\mathcal{I}$ saw Mason leaving, and my father watching him go. I was so excited he'd come. I'd debated sending that invitation. I had to sneak it out in the mail so my father wouldn't see. He had become so protective and overbearing since the crash.

He'd made a complete 180 since that scene in his office so long ago. I guess the thought of losing me changed his priorities. He had moved me back into the mansion until I put my foot down and demanded my own space back in my own apartment. I had my degree. I had a job with his company if I wanted it. He finally agreed to let me leave the mansion after I threatened to join a rival company if he didn't.

Honestly, though, my accomplishments weren't enough. I would give up my dream job if Mason would just come back to me. Working in biotech meant nothing without him.

"Dad, can you drop me off at my apartment? We can do dinner another night." In the passenger seat, I forced a yawn. "I'm really tired."

"Sure," he said. "If that's what you want." He narrowed an eye on me. "Are you feeling well, Kinsey?"

I smiled, but it still felt weird having him worry about my feelings. "Thanks, Dad." I leaned over the gearshift of his Bentley and gave him a one armed hug before hopping out and dragging myself up the stairs to my apartment.

I needed time to figure out how I'd get Mason back. I couldn't survive this separation any longer. Seeing him across the auditorium brought back all those feelings I'd tried so hard to bury. The hurt and want I'd pushed to the back of my mind was front and center once again. I couldn't celebrate my achievement. I couldn't think about anything but him.

I wanted his arms around me. I needed to feel desired. I loved having Dad be the Dad I always wanted, but he was smothering me. I wanted to be treated like a woman, not a child. I wanted to be loved like a woman. I wanted to feel Mason's arms around me again, his hardness inside me again. I needed to feel that wave of emotion crash over me as we sank deeper and deeper into each other again. I wanted to be loved by Mason.

MASON

I dling outside Kinsey's apartment, I tried to work up the courage to go in. I regretted my decision to let Noah chase me away from Kinsey's graduation. That celebration was about her, not me and not Noah. If she'd sent me that invitation, that meant she wanted me there. And I wanted to be there.

Without Kinsey, I was nothing.

I would give it all up to have her. If I had to sell Phantomfire Media I would. If I had to leave my mentor, I would. Kinsey was my everything.

That's it! I'm getting her back.

I stepped out of the car and strode up the stairs to her apartment. Along the way, I sent a quick text to Mark. I had a plan.

Chapter Twenty-Eight

MASON

BANG! BANG! BANG!
"Kinsey?! Open up, Kinsey!"
BANG! BANG! BANG!

*T*he door flew open. "What? Mason, what is it?"
She wrinkled her nose, confused by the wild eyed man standing at her door. My hair stood on end where I'd nervously run my fingers through it for the last few hours. Tie askew, shirt wrinkled, I knew I wasn't the Mason she'd first met. I wasn't perfectly put together with every thread and hair in place. I wasn't perfect at all. She was, though.

"Kinsey," I couldn't speak. I stared into her sparkling eyes, suddenly choking on everything I wanted to say.

She just looked at me, the minutes ticking by.

"Kinsey," I tried again, fighting to find the right words, but they wouldn't come.

Instead of speaking, I grabbed her, pulled her close, and brought my lips to hers. They were impossibly soft. My tongue slipped in between them to tease and play, fighting and sparring, dancing with hers in perfect time. Our chemistry was instant, our attraction irresistible.

Sweeping her off her feet, I carried her into her apartment and kicked the door shut. I cradled her in my arms all the way to the bedroom. There, we collapsed together on her bed, our lips never parting. Suddenly, we exploded in a frenzy of hands and flying clothes as we shed every stitch from our bodies. Skin on skin, I worshiped her, kissing every inch as her head fell back in ecstasy. There was nothing more beautiful than Kinsey lost in the sensation.

"Mason," she said on a breathless sigh. "Mason, I can't believe you're really here. I've dreamed of this."

Our first time in six months was frantic. Our bodies came together, fusing as one, sliding on sweaty skin and bumping as we found our rhythm. My fingers found her center. She was dripping, ready for me.

Sliding between her legs, I stroked her wet opening with my cock, teasing her until she begged. "Mason! Mason, please!" Then I slid home. We fit perfectly, her tunnel warm and tight as I began to move.

We danced like the music had never stopped.

KINSEY

Opening the door and finding Mason on the other side was a dream come true. My mouth grew dry. I had no idea what to say. All the speeches I'd rehearsed fled my mind.

"Kinsey," he said as he stood there gaping.

I wanted to tell him I would give it all up if only he would take me back. I wasn't the same woman he ran into outside my dad's office; I had grown up. With everything I had been through, all we had experienced together, there was no longer any doubt in my mind—I could stand on my own two feet.

But while I *could* do it all, I no longer wanted to. I wanted to walk hand in hand through life with Mason. Together.

"Kinsey," he said again, reaching for me. He pulled me close and lowered his lips to mine.

It was a magical fusing of two souls coming together as one.

～

After, lying blissfully replete, I snuggled into Mason's side. "Come away with me," he whispered. "Let's get married and leave all this behind. I'll sell Phantomfire and join you in your dad's company. You can run it, and I'll support you."

"Mason, no." I was flattered, but it was too much. "You can't give up your company. You've put your heart and soul into it."

"I'll give it all up if it means I can have you." He kissed the top of my head and pulled me closer.

Rolling on to my belly, I propped myself up on his chest and looked into his eyes. "Mason, I would never ask you to give up Phantomfire. I have my degree. I know I can do it, but that's not important to me anymore. What's important is being with you."

"But your father—"

"I don't care." I interrupted his protests with a kiss. "If my father wants me in his life, he will have to accept you too." I kissed him again. I would never get tired of kissing him, feeling our lips connect and the zing of electricity that accompanied our every touch.

"Then I'm taking you away from here for a while," he said.

"Where are we going?"

He smiled. "It's a surprise. You'll see." He ran his fingers through my hair and kissed me again before rolling me over and taking me once more. I had two more orgasms before we were done and he finally let me out of bed.

This time, we traveled over the gulf in first class like when my father and I left Managua. Mason hadn't contracted with a new Gulfstream and crew, and I can't say I was sorry. I was numb when we left Bilwi, and I still wasn't really ready for more small planes.

"Where are we going?" I asked again. I hadn't really paid attention at the airport, still basking in the post coital glow of our reunion.

"I got us a villa on the Emerald Coast. Private pool, beachfront views, spa time for you."

"That sounds amazing!" I snuggled up to his side as best I could in our roomy seats and closed my eyes, letting my mind float away.

Mason had booked us the Casona don Carlos suite at the Mukul resort in Guacalito, Nicaragua. It was an amazing private space—the height of luxury. He had really outdone himself. We even had a butler!

"How was your spa day?" he asked, when I wandered back in from my massage, mask scrub, and some primping. My hair bounced around my shoulders, shiny and full of life, and my nails gleamed with perfect polish.

"I feel so relaxed. It was a fabulous idea to come back here. I had forgotten how beautiful Nicaragua was. Let's go sit on the beach!"

"I have a better idea," he said. "Why don't you put this on?" He opened the bedroom closet door to reveal an intricate white lace gown with mother of pearl beadwork. "Let's go get married on the beach."

I stood there, slack-jawed in my bare feet. I was speechless.

Kneeling in front of me, Mason held up a blue Tiffany's box. He opened the lid to reveal a Tiffany legacy engagement ring. It must have been at least a 2.5 carat center stone. It was beautifully framed by a full circle of bead-set diamonds.

"Mason!" I squealed, bringing my hands to my face, "Oh Mason! Yes, YES!" Jumping up and down I flung my arms around him, raining kisses across his face.

Laughing, we fell backward until I straddled him and our kisses turned passionate.

"Woah," he said, setting me to the side and adjusting his growing hardness, "I would like nothing better than the strip you down and worship your body until you cum for hours, but I meant it when I suggested we go get married on the beach. What do you say? Shall we make this official?"

Crossing my legs, I retrieved the blue box that had fallen to the side as we'd tumbled to the floor. I opened the lid again and marveled at how well he knew me. He had picked my dream ring. The one I surreptitiously googled and dreamt about. I'd sketched that very ring in the margins of my note-books. I'd drooled over it when I ran across similar styles in stores.

"I would love nothing better than to become your wife," I whispered, looking deep into Mason's eyes. "Let's go get married!"

Chapter Twenty-Nine

KINSEY

$\mathcal{H}$olding Mason's hand, we stepped out of the Casona and walked barefoot through the sand to a white wedding arch. Beneath its wind-blown chiffon, we stood to avow our love and commitment by the pristine turquoise waters.

A barefoot priest, his pant legs rolled up, met us, Bible in hand.

"Do you, Mason Andrew Alexander, take Kinsey Bryce Hendrix to be your lawfully wedded wife?"

"I do," Mason replied. "Kinsey, in the beginning, I needed a secretary and you needed a job. My thoughts didn't travel much beyond that. And then I discovered your quirky personality, your joy for life, your passion for learning, and somewhere in the jungles of Nicaragua, I fell in love with you. I love you Kinsey—all of you—the good and the bad. I can't wait to spend the rest of my life with you."

Lost in each other's eyes, he held my hands as the priest turned to face me.

"Do you, Kinsey Bryce Hendrix, take Mason Andrew Alexander to be your lawfully wedded husband?"

"I do," I answered. "Mason, we got off to a rocky start. I was attracted to you and didn't know how to react. I needed a job, and was at loose ends in my personal life. I accepted thinking you would take care of me, but needed to learn to take care of myself. You supported me, and somewhere in the jungle I not only learned how to take care of myself, but I found who I wanted to be. You made that happen, Mason, and I fell in love with you during that journey. Those six months apart were the hardest months of my life. Having you with me is more important than anything else. I love you, Mason."

I don't remember much else. There was a whirlwind of wedding stuff, but I was lost in Mason. We shared an electric connection that swept me away on a river of emotion.

It wasn't until the ceremony was almost over that I realized our family and friends had looked on as we'd cemented our devotion to one another. My Dad had sat to one side with several of his boys. I was surprised to see Damon had come. To his left, a scary military guy I heard him call Liam sat watching, and on his other side, two young men I had only met a few times, Owen and Ryder.

Mark, Laurie, and Mason's mom were there, holding the wiggling twins. And wait! At Mark's feet, was PJ! The last time I called the vet to check, they'd told me PJ had been adopted. I couldn't believe Mason had not only remembered, but tracked him down for me. My life was perfect.

"I now pronounce you man and wife." I heard the words as they floated to me on the wind, and then Mason kissed me. My joy couldn't be contained. It was the first day of the rest of my life with Mason.

Chapter Thirty

MASON

"*M*om wants to know where you are." Mark's voice barked over the phone line.

"We're on our way. Kinsey had to pee three times before we could leave, and then she forgot her back pillow. And then she got hungry, and only an In 'n Out burger would work, so that detour took us 15 miles out of the way. By the time she got her food the dog needed to be walked again. We'll be there soon unless she gets hungry again." I let it all out in a rush.

"Hah! It's your turn, bro!" Mark chuckled, "Laurie was just like that, but worse. We couldn't go anywhere without her suitcase, a packed cooler with snacks, and a map of every clean bathroom on whatever route we were traveling"

"I know every bathroom within a ten mile radius of my house and office!" I exclaimed, laughing into the phone. "We'll be there soon, Mark. Bye." I closed the phone and set it in the console between the seats.

Steering the car through the last bits of traffic, I turned the Range Rover down Mark's long driveway, relieved we had finally made it without stopping again. PJ stood in the back seat, nose pressed to the window.

"Help me down, please, Mason," Kinsey asked, trying to maneuver her bulk around unsuccessfully.

"Here you go." I lifted her out of the passenger seat and gently set her on her feet. At almost nine months pregnant, I wasn't sure coming to the twins' fifth birthday party was a good idea, but Kinsey insisted we couldn't miss it.

"You guys made it!" Mark came out of the house, leading the three of us into the big backyard. The twins immediately claiming PJ and racing around the yard with her.

For the party, Mark and Laurie had set up tents, tables, a bounce house. They'd even brought in a pony.

KINSEY

"Surprise!" Smiling from ear to ear, everyone held up balloons and noisemakers, and someone raised a baby shower banner. Looking around at all the family there, kids screaming, dogs barking my hands flew to my face, and the hormone tears started flowing.

The party could have been a reunion. Mason had invited everyone I ever cared about. "Oh my God! Dad! You're here! And Mason, your whole family! And Mary!" He'd even made sure my old friends from boarding school were there. "Maggie! Harper!"

When I was done kissing and hugging all my guests, Mark's wife led me to the seat of honor under the biggest tent.

"You guys are throwing me a shower? I thought this was a birthday party for the twins!" I looked around, still shocked that this was all for me.

"You're part of the family, Kinsey. Of course this is for you." Mason joined me. He stood at my side, rubbing my back, bringing me a glass of water when I needed it, and handing me things to open. "It's not just you, anymore," he whispered in my ear. "We are all here for you."

"You and Noah are part of the Alexander clan now," Mark said. "We take care of our own."

"Dad?" I called to my father. "I can't believe you are here!"

Walking over and giving me a hug and kiss on the cheek, he nodded. "Of course I came. We spent far too long apart for me to miss this now." Pulling up a chair, he settled in next to Mason. "Besides, I have a shower gift too."

"You?" I said, incredulous. "You brought a shower gift?"

Digging into the inner pocket of his suit coat (no matter how mellow he got, Noah Hendrix, III, did not go anywhere without a fresh suit and tie on), he pulled out some papers.

"I am so proud of you, Kinsey. I know I've never told you, but you have done wonderfully with your life. I let you down after your mother died. I was so worried I would screw something up, I just didn't do *anything*. I didn't know the first thing about raising a teenage girl. I figured the best thing I could do was send you to boarding school and find you a husband to take care of you. I was wrong, and you suffered for it. I want to make it up to you."

Listening to his heartfelt words, I cried again. *Stupid hormones!* I could barely see through the tears to read the papers he handed me.

"What is this????"

"Hendrix BioTech. It's yours. I never should have said it was going anywhere else. I can't think of a better person to run it."

"Congratulations, Kinsey!" Mason said, eyes dancing. *The bastard knew!*

"You knew????" I cried, smacking his arm playfully. I wiped my cheeks as the tears kept falling.

"Of course," he said. "No one loves you more than your father and I. It's our job to take care of you and that baby."

He put a hand on Noah's shoulder. "Besides, Noah wanted to make sure I was on board. We don't want you doing too much with a new baby. He wanted to make sure I would be there for you."

Sobbing, I put my hands over my face. I had never been so happy in my life.

I finally had everything I had ever dreamed of.

THE END

Read ahead for a sneak peek at Damon, Book 2 of Bachelors Incorporated!

Damon, Book 2
Liam, Book 3
Noah, Book 4

Chapter Thirty-One

Sneak Peak

Damon
Bachelors Incorporated, Book 2
Chapter 1

HARPER

*C*RASH!

A tray full of dirty dishes fell and shattered into a million tiny porcelain shards that flew all over the kitchen floor.

"What is going on?!" Nigel stood in the doorway, towering over the new busboy he'd just run into. "What have you done?! You imbecile! I will not tolerate such incompetence here!"

With his shoulders hunched and his eyes downcast, the poor eighteen-year-old kid was quaking in his shoes. I rushed to Nigel, hoping to stop yet another disaster in the making.

"Nigel, calm down. He didn't mean to. You opened the

door on him." I grasped his sleeve and tried to distract him from the dressing-down he was giving Adam. Shit, *that* was a mistake. I knew better than to suggest Nigel ever did anything wrong.

He whirled around and verbally laid into me. "You! You stay out of it! You are nothing but a sous chef! I am the head chef here. You do not contradict me. This is *my* kitchen!" Spittle flew from his angry lips, and his finger jabbed through the air. "Get back to work! We don't have time for your ridiculous excuses and delays."

Throwing a regretful glance in Adam's direction, I scuttled back to my station and began slicing vegetables again. Nigel was not in any mood to be reasonable. For the millionth time, I was glad we were no longer together. *What did I ever see in him?*

Looking sideways at Nigel, I admired his aristocratic profile, aquiline nose, and the way he filled out his chef's coat. His distinguished appearance was what had attracted me to him in the first place. Unfortunately, the beautiful exterior hid a psychopathic narcissist who turned into a tyrant the moment he was given even a tiny bit of power. '

"Faster, Harper." He stood at my shoulder, his critical eye focused on my flying knife as I worked. "I cannot create my masterpieces without proper ingredients. My customers are hungry, and you are slowing things down."

Faster Harper, faster, yada, yada, yada. "MY masterpieces," my foot. These are all my recipes. Bastard is still taking credit for my creations. He doesn't even prepare them—I do!

I fumed as I prepped the vegetables, my knife slicing through the air as I minced, diced, and muttered under my breath. Nigel strutted around the kitchen barking orders at everyone before taking the dishes *I* prepared and delivering them with his pristine white coat and a flourish to the high-profile patrons out in the dining room. What an ass. I couldn't believe I had ever dated him.

All I need's a little more time, and I'll have enough saved up to open my own restaurant. I can survive hell for a little longer, can't I?

DAMON

"Calm down, everybody," I shouted to be heard over the din in the boardroom. Nothing happened. Not one person heard me as I stood there with my hands on my hips at the head of the table, trying to start the meeting. *This is completely unacceptable.*

"ENOUGH!" I finally thundered. My voice rolled around the room, reaching every corner and capturing the attention of every person in the room. Launching myself up onto the conference table, I stood straight, my full 6-foot-five-inches looming over the panicked group. They were going to pay attention to me whether they liked it or not.

More than thirty pairs of eyes turned to look at me, wide and staring as I hovered over them. I don't think they had ever seen a CEO take charge like that. Suddenly all attention was focused on me, previous conversation and bickering forgotten. I could see various reflections of, *Oh shit it's the boss* on each of their faces.

"I am Damon North. The CEO of North Enterprises. This is *my* company, *my* boardroom, and you are all now *my* employees. We will not have a repeat of this little show again. Not ever." I turned a stern glare from one set of frightened eyes to the next, and the next after that. "I expect each and every one of you to conduct yourself with more professional decorum. You are now the face of North Enterprises, and I expect you to act accordingly. This is not kindergarten, and you are not on a playground. You will act like adults. Understood?"

I didn't want to be the heavy, but I also didn't want to spend future meetings standing on tables. We were going to start this new relationship off on the right foot if it killed me.

"I understand you all have a lot of questions, and I will do my best to answer them, but I have a few things to say first. Please be seated." I hopped down from the table and stood at the front of the room, watching as everyone calmed down. This time, they acted like the accomplished individuals I knew them to be, settling into the seats around the room and taking out their pens and notebooks. Within moments, they were all silent and focused back on me again.

"I want to welcome you all to North Enterprises. As part of our latest acquisition, you are the newest members of the North Enterprises family. Melissa?" My right hand and executive assistant Melissa Fielding, who was really so much more than her title implied, began passing out folders. "Inside the folders you are receiving are several documents. You hold the mission statement of North Enterprises; it's why I started the company and how I intend it to continue it. You also have a detailed financial report going back to the very beginning. You will see where I started five years ago and where we currently sit. Please note the robust growth we have and are currently still experiencing. Renewable energy is a hot field and North Enterprises is enjoying unprecedented growth. Please read these documents thoroughly at your earliest opportunity. I expect you to know, understand, and represent the company as it appears in that folder." I pulled out my chair and sat, looking down the long table at all my new employees.

"At the moment, I have no plans to make any significant changes in the company. I wish to see how you run and analyze where your problems are. There will be adjustments in oversight and, eventually, in management. These changes will come months down the road. For now, Melissa and I will be visiting each site and working with each of you individually. I plan to promote Synergy Energy Systems, making it stronger than ever. We will find and fix what led to the fire sale."

The room erupted in chaos again as everyone started speaking at once. Holding my hands up, it took mere moments to hush the crowd again. I must have made a hell of a first impression.

"Each of you here is the director or manager of a department," I said. "I will be meeting with you individually over the next few days to discuss your department and any needs you may have. My assistant Melissa will be scheduling the appointments. Please see her after we are done." I turned and handed the floor to her. "Melissa?"

"Good morning, everyone. I am Melissa Fielding. I will be seated by the door as you leave to schedule your appointments. Here is my business card with my contact information. You are also to call me with any questions or concerns you have in the coming months." She began walking around the room, passing out her cards and greeting everyone.

"Alright," I said. "Let's get this going. You each get two minutes to introduce yourself and tell me your position in the company. You were to block out your entire morning for this meeting. Hopefully, we won't need more time than that. Lunch will be served at one."

I was glad Melissa was here to take notes. By the fourth or fifth person, I realized this was going to be a very tedious meeting. They were all scared about what the acquisition meant for their positions, and each used their two minutes to make themselves sound as indispensable as possible.

A headache began to pound behind my right eye. This was the worst take-over I had ever executed. It had taken three times as long as it should have to get to this point. Usually, I just swooped in, fired everyone, and put my own team in place, but for some reason, I saw something in these people that I thought was worth saving. Although, at that moment, for the life of me, I couldn't remember what I had seen. I needed a break from the madness to recenter myself and get back to what I did best—making money.

∾

"Hey, Mom! I'm here!" I hollered as I let myself in through the front door. Toys and shoes littered the entrance of the small 3-bedroom bungalow. I navigated over and around them to reach the kitchen, the center of everything.

"Hi, honey!" She emerged from the kitchen in the floral apron I remembered from my childhood. As always, a towel hung over her shoulder to dry her hands, and a spot of flour stuck to her face.

She smiled and turned her cheek up to me. I dropped a kiss and gave her a hug, my arms wrapping around her soft middle. She felt like home.

"It's so good to see you!" Over her shoulder, she shouted, "Kids, Damon is here!" At the sound of my name, they all came running.

Seven kids of various ages and Lupita, my foster mom of only two years, lived in the crowded house. I hadn't stayed with her long, but I felt more at home there with her than I had ever felt anywhere else.

"I didn't expect to see you today," she said, sweeping a loose lock of hair from her face. With just a touch of grey at her temples, she didn't look any older than the day I'd shown up on her doorstep with all my belongings in a black garbage bag.

I smiled. "I know. I just kind of felt homesick. I thought I'd come see you guys. Besides, I promised Samantha I'd bring her the next book in the series she's reading." I looked around and found my younger foster sister. She was a tiny thing even at twelve. Her huge glasses adorably overwhelmed her narrow face. Samantha was a voracious reader, and I made sure I always brought her a new book every time I came.

"Do you have it?" She stepped out around her older brother and peered up at me, her blue eyes hopeful behind the thick lenses.

"Yeah, I do." I pulled the paperback from the inside pocket of my suit coat and handed it to her. She took it reverently, admiring the cover before scampering off to her room to devour it. When she was gone, I turned a sad smile to Lupita.

"I know, honey," she said, laying her hand on my arm. "Today's a hard day for all of us. We all remember her."

"Yeah," I whispered, thinking we said the same thing to each other year after year.

Moving into the kitchen, I sat down with them to a lunch of tamales, rice, and beans. They were the comfort foods of my childhood. The faces smiling up at me were different than those I'd shared the table with back then, but their expressions were all the same—sad and hopeful. Just like I had been.

Time passed. Children grew. They changed. I'd changed, but part of me was still the same. Inside me, there was still a boy with a trash bag full of second-hand clothes, looking for a place to call home. Once every month or so, he dragged me back to Lupita's, the closest thing to a home he'd ever found.

"Damon," Lupita asked. "I was wondering if you could help me with something."

"Anything," I said. "What do you need?"

"Carly's class is going on a field trip to Washington."

"D.C.? Oh, that's so exciting!" I smiled at the raven-haired teen as she sat chomping her tamale across from me. "Are you looking forward to it?"

She shrugged. "Lupita says I might not be able to go because we don't have the money." There was no disappointment in Carly's voice. She said matter-of-factly, not once looking up from the book I brought her.

"Ahhh… that's what I wanted to talk to you about." Lupita blushed and looked at her plate. "The electric bill was really high this month. It's been an unusually hot summer, and Joey left his bedroom windows open with the AC on for almost a week. The trip would be so good for Carly. I was wondering…?"

"Sure." I said with a sigh. "I'll call the school and take care of it." Our roles had reversed. I was the one supporting Lupita and the kids now. She was the only mother I'd ever known. I *had* to take care of her.

~

~

Chapter 2

Damon

"I'm telling you, the food here is better."

"No way," I said as we followed the maître 'd. "Nothing is better than the House of Versailles, Melissa. I don't care how good you say it is. It can't possibly trump that."

She shook her head. "I promise—you will love it. Just eat with an open mind."

"Fine." We continued bantering back and forth as we were seated. Opening the menu, I leaned back in my chair and scanned the offerings. "Huh. This does look good."

The menu was varied, offering seafood, chicken, and some prime cuts of meat. All the dishes were prepared with flair, unique blends of flavors and textures.

Of course, Melissa was right as always. Thirty minutes later, I had to admit defeat. "This food is great! I definitely need to add this place to my weekly delivery list. Who's the chef?" I asked, enjoying a sip of the chardonnay I'd ordered to complement my fish.

"Well, this is Harper's restaurant. She's working today, so I'm sure she made our meals." Melissa smiled as she leaned back in her chair.

"Oh ho! You planned this, didn't you? Remind me again, why are we friends?" I grinned cheekily at her.

"You love me, and you know it, Damon. I keep you sane and organized, and all those other things you aren't." She winked. "You know you're like a son to me."

"I know, Melissa, and I love you for it." I paused as the waiter approached to refill our glasses.

"Excuse me." Melissa asked the waiter, "Can you please ask Harper Fielding to come speak with us?"

He nodded in his starched white shirt and black pants, what appeared to be the standard uniform for all the restaurant's employees. "Yes, ma'am. I would be happy to. May I tell her who's asking for her?"

"Yes. Please tell her that her mother and Mr. North are here. Mr. North has been enjoying her appetizers and would like to meet the chef."

"Absolutely. I'll pass on the request and be back in a moment with your salads." He nodded again and sauntered off in the direction of the kitchen.

"Are you sure this is a good idea?" I asked Melissa. "Maybe we should just eat and get back to the office." I was thinking about the stacks of work sitting on my desk. If Melissa had dragged me away from them, I would still be at my desk, plowing through the files. What was another late night after an another ten-hour day?

"Shush, Damon. You needed to eat. Besides, I want you to meet Harper."

I just sighed. There was no sense fighting with the most important woman in my life.

Harper

"Hi, Mom." I bent down to give her a hug.

She kissed my cheek and gave my neck a quick squeeze. "Harper, I would like you to meet my boss, Damon North."

Smoothing back several stray wisps of hair and tugging on the bottom of my jacket, I attempted to make myself presentable in the scant two seconds I had before I turned and smiled at the man across from my mother. Of course he would be drop-dead gorgeous, and I would look like a bag of dog vomit. Sweaty and red-faced with my stringy hair barely contained by a stretched out headband, I was dressed in a limp white coat decorated with a splattered rainbow of spills and drips. I had been on my feet for ten hours already and it showed.

Still, I put my best face forward for Mom. "I'm Harper." I held my hand out to him. "Lovely to meet you."

"Harper, it's so nice to finally meet you. Your mother has told me all about you." He shook my hand confidently, his grip strong, his fingers long and graceful.

"You as well. Are you enjoying your meal?" I clasped my hands in front of me and tried to pretend, in front of the handsome man, that I was a composed professional who was master of her craft—not the failure I felt and looked like.

I desperately needed a cup of hot tea. *I wonder if I could slip away for a few minutes without Nigel blowing a gasket.*

"Absolutely!" He said, though I'd forgotten my own question. "It's wonderful. I'd love to have your restaurant cook for me once a week. Let me know who I should arrange it through." My mind snapped back to the present as Damon handed me a business card, his fingers lightly brushing mine in the process.

"La Maison would be happy to," I said, tucking the card into my coat pocket and hugging my mother one more time. "Mom, I hate to run, but I've got to get back to work before Nigel gets upset."

"Of course, Harper." She put her hand on my arm and grinned. "We'll talk later."

With a nod, I rushed back to the kitchen, my face flushed. I couldn't get away from my mother's boss fast enough. *How could she?* She knew how badly things had gone with Nigel, and how awkward I always felt with handsome men. I scowled. That meeting was not about food; she was trying to play matchmaker.

"Where have you been," Nigel barked at me as I walked through the swinging doors. "We are falling behind. People are waiting. Get back to work."

No tea for me.

"I'm on it." I settled at the grill station and began scooping vegetables and arranging them on a bed of risotto. Then I eased the grilled fish on top, garnished the plate, and slid it down the line. The rhythm of preparing attractive and delicious plates soothed me.

Damon

In my office the next morning, I reviewed the week's meetings with the department heads of Synergy Energy Systems. They were all starting to blur together. Each was passionate about their role in bringing solar and wind energy to the masses and scared to see what I was going to do with their company.

I was convinced renewable energy would be the next big thing, which is why I had taken a chance on buying the failing company and sinking so much of my personal money into making it a success. North Enterprises didn't have a big presence in wind and solar, so adding Synergy to our stable of holdings would bring us into a new, highly-profitable industry.

Truthfully, though, after almost six months of negotiating, closing the deal, and then taking over the company, I was exhausted. I wasn't making good decisions anymore. I needed a break. As I made the decision to walk away for a little while, I felt a huge weight lift off my shoulders.

To get the ball rolling before I could change my mind, I called Melissa immediately and asked her to make the arrangements. "Can you please contact Captain Michael and see if the boat is ready to go out this weekend? I want to take some time off."

"Sure, Damon. Anything else?"

"I'm sure there will be," I said. "Let me know as soon as you get in touch with the captain, please. Oh—and ask him to call me. Oh—and keep an eye on your inbox. I'm going to copy you on the emails I'm sending out with the projects I'm assigning."

"Everything okay?" she asked, concern ringing in her voice.

"Everything's fine. I'm just really tired. It's time for a break."

Leaning back in my chair, I thought about meeting Melissa's daughter the day before. She was beautiful, in a fresh-faced, pure way with no apparent trappings. Face glowing from the steam in the kitchen, she exuded a calm strength. How had I worked with Melissa for so many years and never met her daughter before?

Buzz... Buzz...

I pressed the red button on my intercom. "Yes, Melissa?"

"Damon, I just spoke with Captain Michael. Everything on the boat is ready to go.

"Great! I'll take off in the morning. I'll stay late and rap up what I can tonight." The relief I felt at the thought of getting away was palpable.

"Not so fast," she said. "The boat is ready, but Tom broke his ankle last week and won't be back to work for a couple of months."

I sighed. *There's always a complication.* "Thank you, Melissa. Would you please talk to Michael and see if you can find me a replacement. They will need to be available for at least two weeks.

I took my finger off the button, pulled my phone out of my pocket, and dialed Lupita. "Hey, Mom, can you let Sam know I won't be by for a couple of weeks. I'm gonna take some time off."

I tapped my pen on my desk as she chattered in my ear, her familiar accent comforting.

"Already?" I laughed quietly into the phone. "Okay. Tell her I'll bring her the next book when I get back."

Harper

Sitting at my kitchen table, staring at my empty apartment, I was at my wits' end. Opening the restaurant had consumed my life the last two years, but since breaking up with Nigel the month before, he'd been freezing me out. It seemed he was bent on making my life so miserable I would walk away from my investment. Desperate to make sense of it all, I called the one person I knew could help me sort it out.

"Hey, Mom, I've got a few hours before work. You have time to grab some dinner?" It was a spur of the moment invitation, but seeing Mom always made me feel better. I picked up my mug and brought it to my lips before I realized it was empty, and then set it back down and spun it on the table while we talked.

"I'm so sorry, sweetie." She sounded frazzled. "I'll be working through dinner tonight. It's been pretty crazy around here, and Damon just told me he's taking some time off, so it's just going to get busier."

"You've got to eat. He can't expect you to skip dinner." She had never indicated Damon was that demanding before. "Can I bring you a sandwich or something? I'm so sorry I didn't have time to talk to you a little more yesterday. You know how Nigel is."

The line went silent for a moment before she replied, "I can probably take ten minutes if you can get here soon. It really would be lovely. I don't see you nearly enough, sweetie."

"Okay, Mom. I'll whip something up and be there in thirty minutes." I hung up the phone.

Smiling to myself, I opened my overstuffed fridge and started pulling out ingredients. I hummed happily as I put a pot of water on the stove for tea and set to work. There was nothing that made me feel better than spending time in the kitchen creating something new.

~

"I don't know what to do, Mom. I can't keep working with Nigel." I sat opposite my mother at her desk, several plastic food containers spread out between us. "I thought I could stick it out." I said between bites. "He keeps promising me part of the restaurant. That was the agreement when we started it, but I don't think he'll ever follow through." I stabbed another chunk of roasted asparagus with my fork.

Mom just looked at me as she filled a plate with artichoke pasta salad, roasted vegetables, and the cold braised chicken I'd brought. "This chicken is great. Is it new?"

"Yeah. It's something I've been working on in my free time." I set my fork down and took a sip of water.

"Honey, whatever you decide to do, you know your dad and I will support you." She reached across the desk and took my right hand in hers. "Will you be able to take your recipes with you? I adore that thing you do with fish."

"I don't know. I don't think so. He says the restaurant owns them since I created them while working there." My left hand clenched the water bottle, crunching the plastic.

"I never did like that guy." Mom patted my hand and let go to help herself to more chicken.

"I don't know what to do." I popped a piece of artichoke in my mouth. "I just can't start over. If I leave, I'll be starting from scratch on some lowly prep crew in some second-rate dive. You know Nigel will never give me a recommendation."

And that made me angriest—he claimed all my success as his own. I had been so stupid not to get anything in writing to protect myself.

"You can do it, sweetie. Your cooking is a work of art."

"Thanks, Mom, but they don't take recommendations from mothers. I've got to find a way out that doesn't include restarting my career in the process."

"Oh, Harper, I worry about you." She paused, helping herself to more vegetables, licking her fingers after picking up a beautifully braised artichoke spear and nibbling on it. "You know, I may have an idea. Don't say no just yet, but... um... have you ever thought about being a private chef?" She looked uncertain, and I wondered what she was getting at.

"Yeah," I said slowly, cautiously. "I've thought about it, but people with that kind of money usually hire private chefs from fancy restaurants."

"But it's a viable option, right?"

"Well, unless you are the absolute best, you can't turn it into a full-time gig, so it would be risky. Besides, I want to open my own place. You know that. I—"

"Well, what about for just a few weeks?" she asked, cutting me off mid-sentence. "Damon needs a chef on his boat. He wants to leave this weekend, and his regular chef can't go." She rushed to get the words out before I could argue, her eyes avoiding me as she spoke.

"Mom," I protested, "Damon doesn't want me. Besides, he can cook for himself. His cooking can't be that bad." *How could he want me anywhere around after that embarrassing meeting?* "Anyway, I can't leave my job or be gone for two weeks. If I leave the restaurant, I will need to start looking for something new immediately. I didn't tell you, but..." I bowed my head in shame. "...I loaned Nigel all my money to open La Maison."

"Harper!" She was exactly as disgusted as I'd feared she'd be.

"I know, Mom, I know. It was a really stupid thing to do,

but I was in love—or at least I thought I was." I covered my eyes as they flooded with tears. "He promised me the world, and I believed him. Instead, I lost everything."

She came around the desk and hugged me as I sobbed. "Honey, we'll figure this out. Let me talk to Damon. I really think this might work for both of you."

"Mom," I cried, "why would I want to work for another man?"

Want to read more?
Damon, Book 2

Also by Allison LaFleur

Bachelors Incorporated

Mason, Book 1

Damon, Book 2

Liam, Book 3

Noah, Book 4

Jace, A Novella

(sign up for my newsletter and receive Jace FREE!)

Ryder, Book 7

Luke, Book 8

Whisper Cove

Seaglass Drive, Book 1

Driftwood Lane, Book 2

Shipwreck Road, Book 3

About the Author

I can't imagine a better life than traveling and spinning my stories across all seven continents. I never believed as I child, that writing and publishing would be possible.

I feel so lucky my son and I are able to live in the Florida Keys where I can pursue my dreams. Surrounded by two silly tea cup yorkie pups, we swim, sail, bike, and boat. After work we unwind watching the sun set over the ocean, while I read and write on the porch.

Want to connect with me? Great! I love to hear from my readers. You can find me on Facebook, GoodReads, and the retailer where you bought this book, or simply send an email to:

allison@allisonlafleur.com
or visit
http://www.allisonlafleur.com

CPSIA information can be obtained
at www.ICGtesting.com
Printed in the USA
BVHW071119200319

542953BV00051B/211/P

9 781948 657204